GUILT AT THE GARAGE

GUILT AT
THE GARAGE

Simon Brett

CRÈME de la CRIME

This first world edition published 2020
in Great Britain and in 2021 in the USA by
Crème de la Crime an imprint of
SEVERN HOUSE PUBLISHERS LTD of
Eardley House, 4 Uxbridge Street, London W8 7SY.
Trade paperback edition first published
in Great Britain and the USA 2021 by
SEVERN HOUSE PUBLISHERS LTD.

British Library Cataloguing in Publication Data
A CIP catalogue record for this title is available from the British Library.

ISBN-13: 978-1-78029-132-1 (cased)
ISBN-13: 978-1-78029-740-8 (trade paper)
ISBN-13: 978-1-4483-0468-4 (e-book)

All Severn House titles are printed on acid-free paper.

MIX
Paper from
responsible sources
FSC® C013056

Typeset by Palimpsest Book Production Ltd.,
Falkirk, Stirlingshire, Scotland.
Printed and bound in Great Britain by
TJ Books Limited, Padstow, Cornwall.

To
Ian, Patrick and Alan,
with thanks for their help
in explaining how cars work

ONE

It felt like a personal invasion. Carole Seddon's white Renault was one of her most treasured possessions. Indeed, had she ever been asked to choose between it and her Labrador Gulliver, she might well have come down on the side of the car. And now the Renault had been vandalized. Someone had smashed in the back window. Granulated glass was scattered over the boot space and upholstery.

Carole was appalled. That something like this should have happened in Fethering, of all places! A village of unimpeachable middle-class propriety, minding its own business in West Sussex on the South Coast of England. She wouldn't have been surprised had it happened while she still lived in London, but in Fethering . . . The barbarians really were at the gate.

Under normal circumstances the Renault would have spent the night locked safely in the garage of her house, High Tor. But the evening before, Carole had spent having dinner with her neighbour, Jude, at Fethering's only pub, the Crown and Anchor. She had not exceeded her customary intake of two large New Zealand Sauvignon Blancs but, though High Tor was on the High Street, less than a quarter of a mile away, the law-abiding conformist in Carole had done the responsible thing by leaving her car on the shopping parade and walking home. Jude, being more laid-back about everything, would have assessed the chances of being stopped by police on such a short trip and driven. But Jude didn't have a car, anyway, and, of course, Carole was Carole – a woman in her fifties, thin, spiky, with a helmet of sharply cut grey hair and pale blue eyes that blinked from behind rimless glasses.

She became aware of the vandalism to her Renault the following morning when she took Gulliver for his walk. Carole had recently been experiencing a bit of pain in her right knee, but she wasn't going to allow that to break her established routine. She just stopped more often on the beach while

Gulliver scampered around her. Their regular journey passed the parade of shops. Her plan had been to let the dog stretch his legs on Fethering Beach, and then drive him back to High Tor, but that was before she had seen the smashed window.

Following fast on her initial reactions of shock and affront was one of shame. Carole Seddon had always felt guilty, frequently about things for which she could not possibly have had any responsibility. It was a legacy of her buttoned-up middle-class upbringing. She responded to this tendency towards self-blame by trying never to do anything that might invite censure. She was punctilious in her respect for the laws of the land and also for the more complex societal rules that obtained in a place like Fethering. Though she was not invited out much locally, when she was, she ensured that the reciprocal entertainment she offered was precisely balanced. Though she rarely engaged in conversation with acquaintances she met on her dog walks, she always gave them the minimum greeting of a 'Fethering nod'. Any service from a neighbour, however small, was rewarded with a card of thanks. Though by nature distant and standoffish, Carole Seddon worked very hard not to appear distant and standoffish. Sadly, the outcome of these efforts was only to make her appear even more distant and standoffish.

Carole's nirvana would have been to live in a world where she passed completely unnoticed. But in an English country village, such anonymity is unobtainable.

The shame prompted by the sight of her vandalized car bore this out. The Renault was hers. Everyone in Fethering knew that the Renault was hers. Everyone who saw the smashed rear window would, to Carole's somewhat paranoid mind, be sniggering at her expense. They would be discussing her misfortune behind her back. That, to Carole, would be as much of a personal invasion as the vandalism itself. So, her first priority was to remove the evidence. To minimize the imagined derision from her neighbours, Carole needed to get the glass replaced as soon as possible.

That meant a visit to Shefford's, Fethering's only garage. Though she had bought the car new from a Renault dealer in Brighton, as soon as the free services under guarantee ended, she had transferred her custom to the local man. Bill Shefford had run the garage for as long as anyone in Fethering could remember. Now in his seventies, the general view in the village was that he would soon be handing over the reins to his son Billy, who had worked in the business since he left school. This opinion was unsupported by anything said by Bill himself. The word 'retirement' had never been heard to pass his lips. He behaved like someone who would work for ever.

Carole valued the regular contact she had established with Shefford's. She knew, from uncomfortable experience, how easily women could be patronized by men in the motor trade. Though she would never have claimed any proficiency with machines, she had still felt diminished by the way she had been treated at the Brighton dealership. There had been no overt rudeness, just an underlying don't-you-worry-your-pretty-little-head-about-it attitude which she found distinctly unwelcome.

At Shefford's, though, her ignorance of motoring matters was accepted but not dwelled on. Bill was canny in the management of his mature lady customers. Carole could drop in there with the tiniest anxiety about a flashing warning light and know she would get instant and courteous attention.

He had a particularly good reputation for dealing with the elderly of Fethering. When servicing was due, he would pick up the cars from their homes and return them there. And for those who needed one, a courtesy car was always available. It wasn't a flashy new one with the Shefford's logo on the side, but it was always safe and reliable. And for his less mobile pensionable customers, Bill would personally fill up their cars with fuel, so that they didn't have to get out. He was one of the good guys.

So, Carole's first instinct on seeing her vandalized car was to walk Gulliver back to High Tor – she didn't want him to get cut by shards of glass – then return to the car and drive it straight to Shefford's.

The garage was on the northern edge of the village, just on the edge of the Downside Estate. This sector was made up of what the older and richer residents of Fethering still referred to as 'council houses', though quite a few of them, following Margaret Thatcher's lucrative initiative, were now in private ownership. The younger and richer residents of Fethering described the estate, with just the same kind of snobbery, as 'social housing'. Sadly, because the train line from Fethering to Fedborough, and then on up to London Victoria, followed the course of the River Fether, the Downside Estate could not be described as 'the wrong side of the tracks', but there was a strong feeling among the more genteel residents that it should be.

Most people in Fethering only visited Shefford's to get fuel. The nearest other filling stations were in Fedborough to the north and Worthing to the east. But the garage also offered a repair and parts services, and a fairly low-key second-hand car business, whose offers, with their marked prices behind the windscreens, were lined up on the forecourt. They all looked rather dusty and neglected.

Carole parked the Renault at the end of the used-car row, out of the way of anyone using the petrol pumps. She went to the effort of reversing in, so that the smashed window could not be seen by passing walkers or from cars. Again, she didn't want people gossiping about her.

She went inside to the office, which hadn't changed since the time she had been in Fethering. This was where people paid for their fuel. There was a kind of kiosk, with till and control panel to start the pumps, of which there were only four on the forecourt. The fact that it was not permanently manned showed how slow the trade in fuel was. Not being on the main road, Shefford's customers were mostly Fethering locals – and a lot of those favoured the cheaper prices at the big supermarkets, like Tesco at Littlehampton or Sainsbury's at Rustington.

The room also acted as reception for people bringing their cars in for service. A rather threadbare sofa and a couple of plastic chairs were available for those waiting. There was an antiquated machine which delivered tea and coffee into plastic cups. Having tried its product once, Carole had not repeated the experiment. It was very watery stuff. (Though she had for a long time resisted the current faddishness about the infinite variations with Italian names, even Carole had become pickier about the kind of coffee she drank.)

Though most garages had become minimarkets, Shefford's had not gone down that route. The only items for sale were car-related – plastic containers of oil, light bulbs, wiper blades, cleaning products, de-icers, air fresheners. On the walls were curling posters of other motoring products and a large calendar, provided courtesy of the local Chinese restaurant. Over everything was a patina of dust. It was a while since Carole had been in Shefford's, and she'd forgotten how run-down the whole place was.

The reception area was empty, but through a glass partition could be seen a back office where a woman with unlikely magenta hair was working away in front of a deep monitor whose beige plastic was soiled by oily fingerprints. Beside her keyboard stood a tall desktop computer from another generation. There was access from the room to the fuel payment kiosk. Magenta hair was in charge of that. The other door between the two offices was ajar and the woman looked up at Carole's entrance.

'Can I help?' Her voice was harsh, nasal and loud.

'Yes. Good morning.' Following Fethering convention, though she knew perfectly well who the woman was, Carole didn't use her name. Frankie had done the books and performed various other secretarial duties for Shefford's for as long as anyone could remember. She was older than Carole, so probably round the sixty mark, and unmarried. The fierce red hair was just the latest manifestation of Frankie's urge to draw attention to herself. Changing hairstyles, piercings and tattoos had featured much over the years, and her wardrobe defiantly avoided any two garments that might actually go together. She was a frequent – and loud – visitor to the Crown and Anchor, in the company of a sequence of unsuitable men. She ought to have been a rather sad figure, but somehow contrived not to be.

'Is Bill about?' Carole continued.

'He was here a moment ago. Probably out in the workshop.'

'Would he mind if I . . . .?'

'No, go on through.' Frankie gestured to the door at the back of the reception area.

The workshop was a corrugated-iron-roofed extension which had been there almost as long as the garage. Over the years, the minimum of patching and repair work had been carried out when required, but nothing that would qualify under the title of 'refurbishment'. Carole found the shabbiness rather comforting; for her it exuded an air of unfussy competence. She certainly preferred it to the gleaming and impersonal efficiency of the workshop from which she had collected the new Renault in Brighton.

Hanging from the walls were a variety of tools and equipment, most of whose functions she could only guess at. There were racks of new tyres and electrical appliances. The space was flooded with light; its double doors had been wheeled back, letting in the thin February sunshine. Cars awaiting service, along with a battered recovery truck bearing a peeling 'Shefford's' logo on the side, were parked rather randomly outside against a wire-netting fence.

The workshop had space for two cars to be worked on at a time. On one side a fairly new BMW 1 Series hatchback was raised some six feet above the ground on a still-shiny four-post hydraulic lift; on the other, at ground level, stood a green Morris Traveller. (Carole, whose only interest in a car was: a) that it was a Renault, and b) that it would get her from A to B, could not of course have identified the models with such precision. She would have categorized them as 'one of those flashy German things' and 'an old car with wood on it, like a shooting brake'.)

Apart from the vehicles, the workshop appeared to be empty. Reckoning Bill must be working outside and calling his name, Carole moved towards the doors.

She was surprised to hear, apparently from beneath the ground, his voice asking, 'Can I help you?'

This strangeness was quickly explained, as the garage owner appeared, carrying a torch from the inspection pit beneath the Morris Traveller. He was stocky, pushing seventy, and still had the freckled complexion of someone with red hair. The hair itself, though, was now white and sparse, combed over in inadequate cover.

'Ah. Mrs Seddon. Good morning.'

'Good morning, Bill.' This had been the unspoken protocol since their first meeting. On his instruction, she called him 'Bill', but to him she was always 'Mrs Seddon'.

'What can I do you for?' he asked. It was almost like a catchphrase for Bill Shefford.

'My Renault has been vandalized,' Carole replied dramatically. 'Someone has smashed in the back window.'

'Oh dear. That's bad luck. Where did it happen?'

'On the parade, right here in Fethering!' She still couldn't get over the shock of it.

'Youngsters, I bet,' said Bill wryly. 'Parents don't instil any discipline into them these days, just let them get on with playing all these computer games and sniffing glue.'

Carole gave an enigmatic smile rather than a full endorsement of his view. She didn't want to sound too much like a *Daily Mail* reader. She treasured the superiority of taking *The Times*.

'Anyway,' she asked peremptorily, 'could you sort it out as soon as possible?'

He did that indrawn-breath thing so beloved of doubting workmen. 'Replacing glass is a specialist job, Mrs Seddon. Lots of firms out there who do it.'

'Well, could you organize one of them to come and do my Renault?'

'I could, I suppose, but it'd be just as easy for you to ring them yourself.'

'If you wouldn't mind doing it, Bill . . .?'

The garage owner was used to such appeals from the mature single ladies of Fethering. He pulled a mobile out of his overalls and said, 'See what I can do.' He got through and checked the name of the company.

The person who answered clearly knew his caller well. A time to do the job was offered, but Bill said, 'Oh come on, you can do better than that. It is for one of my special customers.' A concession was clearly made. He ended the call and turned to Carole with triumph. 'They'll be here within the hour.'

'Thank you so much, Bill.'

'One thing, though . . .'

'Mm?'

'Will it be OK with your insurance?'

'I can assure you,' said Carole with an edge of ice, 'that my insurance is fully up to date.'

'I didn't mean that. It's just that some insurance companies will only cover windscreen replacement when it's carried out by a specific repair business . . . you know, one they have an exclusive deal with.'

'My insurance covers everything,' said Carole.

It was agreed that she would go back to High Tor, take Gulliver for his delayed excursion on Fethering Beach, and then walk back to Shefford's. By then, hopefully, the job would be done.

She followed the agreed programme, walking through a part of Fethering she rarely visited. Though close to the Downside Estate, the area had been considerably gentrified. Property prices were high on the South Coast.

When she got home and went into the kitchen, she was surprised to find a sheet of paper, which had been shoved in under the door to the garden. On it had been scrawled, 'WATCH OUT. THE CAR WINDOW WAS JUST THE START.'

TWO

At times, Carole was very good at blanking things out. Like her divorce. With determination, she could spend whole weeks without remembering that she had once been married to David. And that morning, she managed to give Gulliver his freedom on Fethering Beach without considering the implications of the unwelcome gift in her kitchen.

When they got back to High Tor, she found herself hoping, illogically, that the object would no longer be there. But, of course, it was, as unpleasant as a cat's deposit of an eviscerated rodent. And she could no longer stem the flood of thoughts it prompted.

The biggest shock was how that piece of paper changed what had happened to her car. Up until then, she had been affronted by a random attack from Bill Shefford's computer-gaming, glue-sniffing youngsters. Now it had become personal. The perpetrator of the glass-smashing knew who she was, and he or she was planning a campaign of further harassment.

Also, the personal invasion had now extended to her home. In the phrase beloved of gangster movies, the enemy 'knew where she lived'. A gate at the back of her garden led to an alleyway behind the houses of the High Street. It was only locked by a bolt which could be easily reached from outside. Someone had opened the gate and crossed her back garden to stuff the missive under the door to her kitchen. Knowing that was not a nice feeling.

Carole needed to be busy. She always needed to be busy, to keep unpleasant thoughts at bay. And her current thoughts were so unpleasant that she need more than ever to be busy. She checked her watch. Less than an hour had elapsed since she left Shefford's. The windscreen repair man would hardly have arrived at the garage, let alone finished the job. It was the perfect opportunity to sort out the insurance.

The documents were neatly filed in her upstairs study, which had been designed by the architect who built High Tor as a second spare bedroom. And it was occasionally used as such, on the rare occasions when her son Stephen, daughter-in-law Gaby and two adored granddaughters, Lily and Chloe, all came to Fethering at the same time. Then the adult visitors would stay in the twin-bedded spare room and the little girls would sleep on fold-out mattresses in the study.

Everything in her workspace was neatly filed. It was a legacy from the time Carole had spent working at the Home Office. There, she had been constantly commended for her efficiency and in her Fethering retirement, though there was no one to witness it, she still prided herself on that efficiency.

Her filing cabinet stood to one side of the table on which sat her laptop. The machine, whose purchase had been long resisted but was now an essential part of Carole's life, had rarely had its portability put to the test. She treated it like a desktop computer. Inside her compartmentalized mind, doing things online was an activity to be pursued in her study, not in any other part of the house. And the laptop was certainly never used for entertainment, music or television streaming. Its exclusive purposes were the sending of emails and the occasional fact-checking foray into Wikipedia.

Practical activities, like contacting insurance companies, also belonged in the study. The downstairs phone and the bedside one, on the same landline, were used for social purposes, which meant not very often (except for calls to the Fulham home of Stephen, Gaby and the granddaughters). Carole Seddon's mobile was rarely used at all, and certainly not when she was inside High Tor. As she would say tartly, if asked about the subject, 'I am not of the generation that needs to consult their screen every five minutes.' Everything within Carole Seddon's life had very strict rules.

But she was soon going to have to bend or extend her rules in relation to the mobile. Gaby had recently set up a family WhatsApp group, on which Carole received treasured photos and videos of the grandchildren. Lily and Chloe would be coming to stay on their own for a weekend in March and Carole was very much looking forward to their visit. So much so that she had spent a whole weekend redecorating the spare room where they would stay. She had covered the old magnolia emulsion on the walls with a more girly pink, but not been so bold with the gloss on the door, window frames and skirting board. They had been repainted white as before. The project had been hard work because Carole was – no surprise – a very meticulous decorator. She sanded down the old paint on the wooden parts, filled in the crevices with Polyfilla, then used primer and gloss. For the skirting boards, this mean a lot of getting up and down off her knees. Her body felt the effects for a good few days. But she was very pleased with the result and couldn't wait to see the little girls' reaction.

By the time they came, she was determined to be a proficient contributor to the family WhatsAppery, so that she could send photos and videos of her granddaughters' activities back to Fulham. As a result, Carole had started very tentatively teaching herself how, for the first time, to use the camera facility of her phone.

She quickly discovered that the mobile she had was far from state-of-the-art. The cameras on newer phones were much more sophisticated. They had more pixels, whatever they might be. So, Carole didn't get rid of her old phone but she did buy a new one, which would take better photos and videos. She had ordered it online but did not want to let it be seen in public until her mastery of it was complete. In fact, so far, she hadn't taken it out of the box.

But she wasn't going to use either mobile that morning. From the landline in her study she rang the claims line of her insurance company. Once she had gone through the process of identifying herself and giving her policy number, she announced, 'I have been the victim of vandals who have smashed in the back window of my car.'

'I'm very sorry to hear that,' said the Northern female voice at the other end of the line. The sympathy was automatic, impersonal. 'Have you reported the incident to the police?'

'No, I haven't.'

'Well, you'll have to. We'll need a Crime Number before we can process your claim.'

'Oh.'

Carole must have sounded deflated, because the girl said, 'It's a very simple process.'

'I'm sure it is.'

'You don't dial nine-nine-nine, though. You dial one-oh-one.'

'Yes, I know that,' said Carole testily. Although she didn't. The person she was talking to had no idea her caller had ever worked for the Home Office, but Carole still never liked to admit ignorance on police matters.

'Get back to us when you've got the Crime Number and then we can proceed and put you in touch with one of our authorized windscreen repair services.'

'But I've already arranged to have the glass repaired. I can't leave my car open to anyone who wants to help themselves to the contents.'

'Are you saying that you keep valuables in your car? Because if you do, we would recommend that you remove them as soon as possible.'

'That's not the point. The point is that the glass is already being repaired.'

'May I ask the name of the company that is effecting that repair?'

Carole supplied the name that Bill Shefford had given her.

'Can you just hold for a minute, Mrs Seddon?' There was a long silence, but not, mercifully, long enough to be filled by music. Then the girl came back on the line. 'I'm very sorry, Mrs Seddon. I'm afraid that is not one of the companies authorized by us.'

'So, what are you saying?'

'I am saying that, if you get your glass repaired by that company, your insurance with us will not cover the expense.'

Carole could think of a lot of responses to that, many involving expressions like 'cartel', 'restrictive trade practices' and 'mutual back-scratching'. But she did not give any of them voice. She simply rang off, seething with fury.

Most of that fury, of course, was addressed to herself. She knew what she should do. The windscreen repairer summoned to Shefford's probably hadn't even started on the job yet. She should ring Bill and put him off. Then she should dial 101 and get a Crime Number. She should also tell the police in that call about the unpleasant message still lying on her kitchen floor. She had, after all, been deliberately targeted by a criminal.

But, because she was Carole Seddon, she did none of these things. Because all of them would have drawn public attention to her shortcomings. She should have known about the limitations of her car insurance. Or at least she should have checked its provisions before she authorized the repair. And someone who had spent most of her career at the Home Office should have known the right thing to do was to report the crime.

But all Carole could think was that, if she allowed the repair at Shefford's Garage to continue, very few people would ever know about her Renault having suffered the indignity of being vandalized. Bill Shefford, yes, but no one else at the garage.

The repairman would know nothing about the circumstances of the breakage. Inevitably, a few locals taking early morning walks past Fethering Parade would have recognized her car. But only a few. Hopefully, her prompt action would have staunched the noxious flow of village gossip at source.

The next thing she did, Carole knew was wrong by any standards. She picked up the piece of paper on the kitchen floor, got out a box of matches and burnt it in the sink. She washed the ashes down the plughole. She shuddered slightly as the last black flakes disappeared.

Her fear of doing something wrong was not as strong as her fear of drawing attention to herself.

Carole Seddon was very good at blanking things out.

She continued with her morning as if the call to the insurance company had never happened. Gulliver stayed at High Tor beside the Aga, trying on the reproachful look of a dog who hadn't just been for a nice gambol on Fethering Beach. The reproach was mixed with resignation. Long experience had taught Gulliver that he very rarely got more than his scheduled morning and evening walks. But it was worth trying, hope once again triumphing over experience.

The only difference when she got back to Shefford's was that the Renault had been moved. Presumably, that meant the repair work had started and was being done round the back of the building. Inside the reception area, there was no one around, not even Frankie in her glass box. Carole moved towards the workshop door, which was ajar. She was about to go through when she was stopped by the sound of a voice raised in anger.

'But, for God's sake, you've got to make a decision soon!'

She recognized the tones of Billy, Bill Shefford's son and – everyone in Fethering assumed – his father's partner in the business.

'I don't want to be hasty,' responded Bill, clearly not enjoying the confrontation.

Carole moved to sit on one of the plastic chairs, the optimum eavesdropping position.

'We can't just let things drift on,' Billy persisted.

'They've been "drifting on" – as you put it – quite satisfactorily for nearly forty years.'

'Yes, but times have changed, Dad. You don't seem to realize how much times have changed.'

'Just give me time to think about it, Billy.'

'You've had bloody years to think about it, and you've still got no nearer a decision!'

'Don't shout. The windscreen repair guy will hear you.'

'I don't care who hears me! You know when Mum was alive, she kept saying that you should make changes. She's been gone seven years and what's happened? Bugger all.'

'Hm. Valerie always did spoil you.'

'What's that got to do with anything? I'm talking about saving this business.'

'I'll think about it,' Bill Shefford insisted feebly.

'Oh yeah? After you've consulted *her*, no doubt?'

'Obviously, I won't make decisions on something as major as this without consultation.'

'"Consultation"? The person you should be consulting is not *her*. It's me, your bloody business partner!'

There was a silence after this outburst. Then a new voice joined the discussion. Frankie's. 'And what's this about her doing a book-keeping course?'

'The education system wasn't so good where she grew up. She's got a lot of catching up to do.'

'Oh yes?' Frankie's voice was larded with cynicism. 'Sure you're not lining her up to take over my job?'

'I wouldn't do that, Frankie. You know I wouldn't.'

'Wouldn't you? You'd do anything she tells you to.' The cynicism in Billy's voice was laced with pain. 'And why didn't you tell me she was doing a car-maintenance evening class as well as the book-keeping? Thinking she'll be able to replace me too, are you?'

'Billy, son, you know it's not like that. I do have some concept of loyalty.'

Carole looked up at the sound of the garage's front door opening. A short, rather beautiful woman of Asian origin entered, just as Billy said, 'And what kind of loyalty did you show to Mum's memory by marrying *her*?'

'Ah,' said the new arrival, in very slightly accented English. 'They are talking about me.'

THREE

Jude, Carole's neighbour, was, as the French say, a woman who fitted her skin. And with the passage of the years, there was no lack of skin to fit. The precise definition of her contours was vague, because her dress style always involved a lot of floaty garments and light scarves. In the same way, the contours of the furniture in her sitting room were softened by a plethora of rugs and throws. Jude's blonde hair was always piled up on top, secured in a gravity-defying structure of grips and pins. There was a natural warmth about her which, for men, invariably translated into sexual magnetism.

Jude was a healer whose sitting room in Woodside Cottage was her treatment space. She worked to her own timetable. Though she would be there for anyone in a crisis, she generally didn't book in any appointments before ten in the morning. She liked the waking-up process to be gentle, and faced the world more happily after a cup of tea in bed.

But receiving a phone call at nine thirty that morning seemed quite acceptable. It was not from someone she recognized, a man who identified himself simply as 'Jeremiah'. (Given her own reluctance to use any of her surnames, Jude could hardly blame him for that.)

'Good morning. My name is Jeremiah, and I am a healer.'

'Ah. Good morning, Jeremiah.'

He had a deep, confident voice which she was sure could sound very empathetic in a therapy situation. 'I've recently returned to this country after practising in the States and Australia for some years. Well, since I've been working in this area, everywhere I go I'm told that the go-to local healer is someone called Jude in Fethering.'

Unsure whether this was just flannel, Jude said nothing, so Jeremiah went on, 'Anyway, a) I'd like to meet you, and b) I have an idea for a project on which I would be interested to get your views.'

Jude was wary of 'projects', particularly when put forward by other people in the therapeutic world. Too often, they involved some collaborative venture and, though Jude was very open to other people, she knew that her healing was only effective when she did it on her own. The concentration of energy she asked of herself was never so easy to summon up when there was a person other than her client present. But it would have been churlish to refuse to meet Jeremiah. Over the years, she had made a lot of friends through the business of healing and complementary medicine. Jude was a great believer in learning from other people.

So, she invited Jeremiah to join her for coffee at Woodside Cottage. He was going to be away for most of the next week but they fixed a date after that.

'As you know, I don't like gossip,' Carole lied.

'No?' said Jude. 'The only gossip you don't like is the kind someone else heard before you did.'

Carole didn't think this childish (if accurate) barb was worthy of response, so she just listened as her neighbour went on, 'I'm surprised you haven't heard, though. It's been round Fethering for months. The woman you met at the garage is called Malee. She's Bill Shefford's second wife. They married . . . I don't know, eight months ago . . . might even be a year now.'

'And where does she come from?'

'Thailand.'

'Good heavens. A "Thai Bride"?' Carole breathed the words with appropriate tabloid awe.

'If you want to call it that, I suppose she is, yes.'

'Well . . .'

They were sitting in the cluttered front room of Woodside Cottage, a nest of soft furnishing, of rugs and throws. For her clients, Jude's healing process started the moment they entered the nurturing ambience of her home.

'What you're saying,' Carole went on, 'is that Bill Shefford's got a "Mail Order Bride"?'

'You may be saying that. I'm not. Bill did actually meet Malee when he was on a trip to Thailand.'

'So, what difference does that make?'

'I think a "Mail Order Bride" is generally considered to be someone who registers themselves with an international marriage agency, hoping to attract a husband from a wealthier country. That's not what happened with Bill and Malee. They met socially while he was on holiday in Thailand.'

'When you say "socially", you don't mean they met at a cocktail party, do you?' asked Carole beadily.

'No, probably not. Bill went out to Thailand on a group tour. He met Malee. A few weeks later she came to England and they got married at the registry office in Fedborough.'

'So, what was Malee doing in Thailand at the time they met?'

'I think she was a waitress in the hotel where he was staying.'

'Then it's the same difference really, isn't it, Jude? She might as well have been a "Mail Order Bride". She was on the lookout for a wealthy Englishman to get her out of poverty, and he was looking for a continual supply of subservient sex.'

For an intelligent woman who did *The Times* crossword, Carole often came across as surprisingly *Daily Mail*. 'From all I can gather,' Jude said, 'it's turned out to be a very happy marriage.'

'Huh,' said Carole, as only she could say 'Huh.' She went on, 'Well, I didn't get the impression Bill's new bride was spreading much sweetness and light into the next generation.'

'Billy?'

'Yes.'

'Hm.' Jude nodded. 'Billy's a man with problems.'

'Oh? And, incidentally, how is it that you know so much about the Shefford set-up?'

'I've been doing some work with Billy's mother-in-law.'

'By "work", I assume you mean "*healing*"?' Carole could never keep a shade of contempt out of her pronunciation of that word. But then again, she didn't really want to keep it out. To her, any form of medical procedure that didn't involve an NHS GP was deeply suspicious. The very word 'healer' carried with it an ineradicable whiff of charlatanism.

'Shannon Shefford's mother, Rhona, is dying.'

'Oh, and you can heal her of that, can you?'

It was a cheap shot, but Jude didn't rise to it. She just said, 'I can perhaps make her last months less stressful.'

'Huh,' said Carole. But she did feel slightly guilty for the cynical line she had taken. She often made pronouncements that came out sounding more callous than she'd intended. She envied her neighbour's skill for saying the right thing at the right time.

A sudden twinge of pain in her right knee distracted her. She adjusted her position in the armchair as subtly as she could, but Jude still noticed.

'Something wrong with your leg?' she asked.

'No, no,' Carole responded hastily. 'Just a touch of cramp.' The last thing she wanted was her neighbour offering to heal her.

Jude didn't believe the answer. She'd noticed Carole limping slightly the last few weeks. But she moved the subject on. 'Oh, incidentally . . .' said Jude, 'sorry about your car.'

Carole was incensed. 'How did you know about that? Did you see it down at the parade this morning?' That seemed unlikely. She knew Jude did not share her strict regime of early rising.

'No, no,' Jude replied. 'I heard about it from a friend in the village.'

Carole curbed the instinctive urge to ask which friend. Though she did very much want to know, she didn't wish to sound needy. In all areas of her life, she expended a lot of energy in trying not to sound needy. Also, there was an element of jealousy in her reaction. Jude found meeting new people so much easier than she did. Carole didn't want to hear further proof that her neighbour was friends with more Fethering residents than she was (even though Jude hadn't lived in the village nearly so long).

'Yes, it was unfortunate,' said Carole. 'There's far too much random vandalism around these days.'

'Surely better to have random vandalism than targeted vandalism.'

Carole looked sharply at her neighbour. Jude couldn't be implying . . .? But the brown eyes looked so innocent, she knew the remark had had no hidden agenda.

For a moment, she felt strongly tempted to tell Jude about the note that had been shoved under her kitchen door. Its appearance had affected her more than she cared to admit to herself. And Jude always offered a sympathetic ear – indeed, much of her job description required offering a sympathetic ear. But no, Carole didn't want to involve her. Some illogical voice within her said that if she told no one about what had happened, the threat would go away.

'Anyway, I've had it repaired,' she announced briskly. 'The Renault is safely back in the High Tor garage.'

'Good. And presumably, everything was covered on your insurance?'

'Oh yes,' said Carole airily.

'Of course, Shannon should have gone to university,' announced Rhona Hampton.

'Uhuh,' said Jude, only half concentrating on her client's words. Her main focus was on healing, channelling its power into the frail body lying on the bed. The covers had been pulled back but Rhona had kept her nightdress on, accentuating the pathetic thinness of her mottled arms and legs. Jude just ran her hands slowly along the body's contours, not touching, translating the energy into comfort.

Both women knew there was no hope of a cure for Rhona's liver cancer. Jude's mission was palliative care. That was accepted between them. The old woman never talked of death, so Jude didn't either. Some people in the last stages of her life, she knew, were terrified, some remained endlessly curious, others ignored their situation. Her job was to adjust to the needs of the individual client.

The request for her services had come from Shannon who, it turned out, was a great believer in alternative therapies. And Jude reckoned it must have taken quite a bit of persuasion for Rhona to agree to the treatment. Shannon's mother seemed very old-school and traditional, probably of Carole's view that all medical needs could – and should – be supplied by the

NHS. And Shannon said she'd tried to get another alternative therapist to work with her mother, but after ten minutes he'd been denounced by the old woman as a 'snake-oil salesman'.

Shannon had, however, done the groundwork somehow, because Rhona did agree to let Jude come and see her. Maybe it was a gender thing. The old woman didn't like being treated by a man. Shannon said she thought that was probably it. In future, she'd always recommend a male therapist for a man, and a female for a woman. Jude, whose experience did not support that approach – she had had an equal success rate with clients of both genders – had not taken issue about it.

At their first encounter, Rhona was very suspicious, but Jude's easy manner had worked its customary magic. Since then, the old woman had expressed strong views on many subjects but she hadn't said a word of disparagement about alternative medicine.

That day she and Jude were in the downstairs front room of the younger Sheffords' house, an unimaginatively designed seventies four-bedroomed number called, for no very good reason, Waggoners. Ideal for a young couple with two infant sons, which is what Billy and Shannon had been when they bought it. Whether the house was quite so suited to accommodating a dying mother-in-law, as well, was a subject on which Billy had been heard to express views after a couple of pints in the Crown and Anchor.

Certainly, in the eight months since Shannon had decided her mother could no longer manage in her own flat, Rhona's presence at Waggoners had caused visible disruption. For a few weeks, she had been allocated the spare room, between the two boys' bedrooms on the first floor. But the stairs soon became too much for her to cope with, and Shannon had declared that her mother must have the front room, formerly the family sitting room. The change required a certain amount of DIY input from Billy. New shelves were needed to fit around the pieces of furniture Rhona had brought with her from the flat. A handrail had to be erected by the step up to the front door (though it became increasingly rare for the old lady to go outside the house). More rails had to be fixed in the hall on the route to the downstairs lavatory, and some inside the lavatory itself, which was now designated for Rhona's exclusive use.

All of this work Billy Shefford undertook without complaint, though occasionally Jude got the impression he was asking himself if it was really necessary. It was, after all, only a matter of time before all of these geriatric aids would need to be removed. But, from her observations of Billy and Shannon's marriage, Jude got the impression that such reservations would never be voiced.

Shannon had always adored her mother – 'I love her to bits' she kept saying – and that unalterable fact Billy had had to take on board right from the beginnings of their relationship. Those beginnings went a long way back. Billy and Shannon were childhood sweethearts. They had got together at the comprehensive in Clincham when they were both fourteen, and neither had had eyes for anyone else since. They had married four years later; 'far too early', in the opinion of Rhona, who was still going on about it that morning while Jude was treating her.

'Shannon was definitely university material,' she repeated. 'Her teachers at the school said that. She could have gone on and got a proper qualification, rather than tying herself down with a *garage mechanic*.'

Jude had heard the contempt in the last two words many times before, but never made any comment. Rhona thought her beloved only daughter had married beneath her, and nothing would change that opinion. Jude felt considerable sympathy for Billy. He had accepted the mother as part of the package when he took up with the daughter. He had known Rhona would always be critical of him, but now the critic was firmly embedded inside his own house.

Jude decided to put up a minor defence of the poor man. 'He's a bit more than a garage mechanic now, Rhona. He and Shannon have a very enviable lifestyle.'

This was greeted by an entirely predictable, 'Huh. Shannon could have done a lot better for herself on her own. If she'd gone to university, she could have become a lawyer or something like that. Moved in professional circles, ended up marrying someone who was more on her sort of . . . intellectual level. They make a lot of money, top lawyers, you know. Much more than garage owners.'

'Well, from what I've seen of them together,' said Jude, palliative in more ways than one, 'Shannon and Billy seem to have a very happy marriage.'

'Appearances can be deceptive,' said Rhona darkly.

It struck Jude for the first time that maybe the old woman's antipathy for her son-in-law arose from a dislike of men. All men. Jude had never heard any mention made of Shannon's father. Had he abandoned Rhona with a young baby, leaving her to bring Shannon up on her own? And had that betrayal sparked in Rhona a distrust of the entire gender? It was a mildly interesting speculation but, Jude reminded herself, not really her business. Her sole function at that moment was to alleviate the discomforts of a dying woman.

And Rhona's sole function at that moment – as at many other moments – seemed to be to continue criticizing her son-in-law. 'Anyway, I'm not sure Billy's future's that secure at the moment.'

'Oh?'

'He's worked for his dad all these years and everyone reckoned that, when Bill finally retired, the son'd take over. After Valerie died, Bill made a will leaving the business to Billy. But is that still going to happen now his dad's taken up with this Chink?'

Jude, careful not to show any reaction, winced inwardly. Rhona's generation were not great exponents of political correctness. All she said, mildly reproving, was, 'Malee's from Thailand.'

'Thailand, China, they're all the same. Can't trust Asians. Gold-diggers, money-grubbers, the lot of them.'

'I don't think you're being fair, Rhona. You can't condemn a whole nation like that.'

'Why not? I speak as I find. And I know that this Molly, or whatever she's called, is only after Bill Shefford's money.'

'You can't be sure of that.'

'Oh no? So, tell me . . . what else is going to make a balding, overweight seventy-year-old man attractive to a girl in her twenties?'

'I think Malee is actually older than—'

'Poppycock! She's got her claws into Bill all right. She only lets him out of her sight to go to the garage. She's cut him off from all his old mates. Bill used to go fishing every Sunday with his chum, Red. He did that back when Valerie was alive. Him and Red had been at school together, with Valerie and all. I always liked Red – nice boy. Very fond of Valerie, he was. Shy man, could seem a bit standoffish, but always very polite to me. Not, of course, that I've seen him recently.

'Because, you know why? Has Bill been fishing once since *she*'s been on the scene? No. She's put a stop to that. Which means of course I don't get to have a natter with Red. Which I always enjoyed. He and I think alike on most things.

'But oh no, we don't see Red now. *She*'s jealous of Bill seeing other people, afraid someone will put him right about who he's actually got himself mixed up with. A gold-digger. She's only ever been after Bill's money and all she wants to do is diddle Billy out of his inheritance!'

Fortunately, further pirouettes in this circular argument went prevented by the appearance of Rhona's daughter. Shannon Shefford was a tall, well-muscled woman in her late forties. Her blonde hair was pulled back into a ponytail and she wore a no-nonsense T-shirt and jeans.

'Hi, Jude. Hello, Mum, how're you doing?' Instinctively, she bent down to kiss the wrinkled cheek.

'Mustn't grumble,' said Rhona. Then, after a well-judged pause, 'Though, of course, I do. But I don't need to tell you that.'

Her daughter's presence had had an immediate effect on the old woman, mellowing, making her less spiky. Shannon's love was clearly reciprocated.

She used to work as a legal secretary for a solicitor in Fedborough but had given up when Rhona had to move into Waggoners. She was now a full-time carer for her mother. Whether that put pressure on the family income, Jude didn't know. Certainly, she never heard the subject mentioned.

Mother and daughter were so used to Jude's presence in the house that, having acknowledged her, Shannon continued as though there was no third person present. Jude just got on with her palliative care and listened.

'God,' said Shannon, 'there are some bloody stupid people out there.'

'What, is this the meeting you've just come from, love?'

'Too right, Mum. You know, I told you it was a fundraising committee for the Green Party and, like, we were throwing around some ideas for making money and this one elderly idiot – I don't know what his name is but he's clearly got more money than sense – anyway, he suggests raising sponsorship for some trip he's taking. OK, what kind of trip, we ask. And he only tells us that it's some big rally – hundreds of SUVs driving from London to Saudi Arabia or somewhere. And he says he's got lots of wealthy chums who'd sponsor him to complete the course and raise lots of the old mazuma. That's what he actually said – "lots of the old mazuma". Where did he get that from? And I say, "You do know who we're trying to raise money for, don't you?" And he says, "Yes. The Green Party." And I say, "Duh. Don't you see something kind of wrong about raising money to protect the environment by driving highly polluting vehicles for thousands of unnecessary miles?" And he just doesn't get it. He gets all shirty and says, "I was only trying to help. I do have some very well-heeled friends who could do your cause a lot of good", and he looks at me like I've just strangled his favourite puppy. What an idiot! I just cannot bloody believe it.'

'They don't understand people with principles, do they? And you've always had principles, haven't you, Shannon?' Rhona condescended to include Jude in the conversation. 'Right from when she was a little girl, Shannon had principles, you know. It was about animals then. Shannon couldn't bear to see an animal hurt. Could you, Shannon?'

Shannon agreed that she couldn't.

'Used to save up your pocket money to give to the RSPCA, didn't you, love?'

Shannon agreed to this too.

'And then, as she got older, Shannon realized that doing harm to animals was part of something much bigger, which was doing harm to the environment. And now she devotes a lot of time and energy to the Green Party. You do, don't you?'

Shannon could not deny it.

'Which obviously makes her domestic situation very difficult.'

'Sorry? Why?' If Jude was going to be part of the conversation, she might as well ask when she didn't understand something.

'Well, you see, her marriage . . .'

'There's nothing wrong with my marriage,' said Shannon, in the weary tone of someone who has rehearsed these arguments many times before.

'You say that . . . and you're always very loyal to Billy . . . more loyal, to my mind than you need to be . . . but the fact remains that you're now in an impossible moral situation.'

'Mum, it isn't a case of—'

'Like I always say, if you'd gone to university, you could be a lawyer now, not just a secretary. You could be a lawyer specializing in taking to task all those multinational petrochemical companies . . .' The alternative life Rhona had built up for her daughter didn't lack for detail. 'Then you could feel that you're doing some good. Which, of course, you can't, having got married so early . . .'

'Mu-um . . .' said Shannon plaintively

'. . . and marrying someone whose work involves supporting the petrochemical industries. Selling petrol, for a start, and then repairing cars and encouraging people to go out and spread pollution all over the place.'

'Mum, please. Jude doesn't want to hear all this.'

The Jude in question didn't mind, actually. She was permanently curious about her fellow human beings, and constantly amazed by the diversity of their interests and behaviour. The work she did gave her unrivalled access to the lives of others.

'Well, I speak as I find,' said Rhona. Her daughter's reaction showed it was another line she heard with considerable frequency.

But Rhona hadn't finished needling. She should have realized by now that nothing she said was going to bring down her daughter's marriage, but she still had to keep chipping away at its foundations. 'You know Billy's plans for the garage, don't you?'

'Yes,' said Shannon wearily.

'He was talking to me about them only yesterday,' Rhona persisted. 'He makes no secret of them. One of my Fethering friends heard him sounding off about them in the Crown and Anchor. When he gets control of Shefford's, he wants to turn it into a dealership with one of the big companies; a foreign one – Nissan, Toyota, Honda, one of those Eastern ones. Billy reckons that's where the money's going to be in the future. He says there's no profit in filling cars with petrol and doing repairs.'

'Mum . . .' said Shannon with a long-suffering sigh, 'Billy's told me all this. I know what his plans are.'

'Yes, but Jude doesn't know, does she?'

Jude thought it rather strange that she was being brought in to help in the demolition of Rhona's son-in-law. It wasn't a position she particularly relished, but she kept quiet.

'Anyway, it's all going to change soon,' said Shannon.

'What's all going to change?'

'The motor industry. In twenty years' time, there won't be any fossil fuels. If Billy does get his dealership, he won't be selling petrol-driven cars. They'll all be electric.'

'So they say,' Rhona intoned darkly. 'The politicians. Mind you, politicians will say anything if it's going to squeeze out one more vote for them.' Shannon's face suggested this was also a view she'd heard expressed many times before.

Her mother went on the offensive again. 'And how do you reckon your Billy will manage, converting Shefford's to all-electric? He's never been good at change, has he?'

'He'll cope,' said Shannon. 'Anyway, the future at the garage is all rather in the air at the moment.'

'Oh yes,' said Rhona. 'Since Billy's dad married the Chink, you mean?'

As she left Waggoners, Jude could not help feeling a surge of sympathy for Billy Shefford, caught in a pincer movement between a wife who disapproved of the work he did and a mother-in-law who disapproved of him full stop.

No wonder he spent a certain amount of time sounding off in the Crown and Anchor.

FOUR

Carole's skills at blanking things out were finite. However determinedly she tried not to think about the attack on her Renault, nagging anxieties kept on invading her mind. It wasn't the smashed glass that caused them – she had come to terms with that – it was the note through the kitchen door, the note that changed a random act of violence into targeted aggression. The temptation to talk about it, to tell Jude what had happened, was strong. Except, of course, that would probably have meant owning up to her inefficiency over the car insurance. Not to mention her stupidity in burning the vital evidence. No, she'd have to bottle it up. And Carole Seddon was very practised in bottling things up.

She was also very practised in being slow to change her habits. Everything new she approached with suspicion. For many years, she had resisted computer technology. It was the same with mobile phones and, currently, using the camera function.

Then again, for a long time, when in Jude's company, the two of them had drunk Chilean Chardonnay. And when they came to the mutual conclusion that Sauvignon Blanc was much nicer, it still felt wrong to Carole. Although she wondered how they had apparently enjoyed the Chardonnay for so long, she did feel a pang almost of betrayal at a bar when ordering Sauvignon Blanc.

It was the same with coffee. Carole's instinctive Englishness and aversion to change had made her very suspicious of the invasion by coffees with foreign names. Resolutely resisting the siren calls of mochas, lattes and macchiatos, when offered a choice she would reply stuffily, 'Just ordinary black coffee, please.' And when Polly's Cake Shop on the parade closed, Carole's voice was strong in condemning the prospect of its being replaced by a Starbucks. The very idea was appalling. This was Fethering, after all. Fethering would never give way to the relentless march of the multinationals.

But, of course, Fethering, like so many other places, did give way to the relentless march of the multinationals. And, though Carole at first condemned the fickleness of the locals who immediately flooded into the new Starbucks, she did occasionally find herself ending up in there. She had even been heard to order, 'A black Americano, please.'

There wasn't a regular pattern to when she went out for coffee. Apart from mealtimes, the two fixed points of Carole's day were Gulliver's walks on Fethering Beach – as soon as it was light in the mornings and just before it got dark in the evenings. She had bought the dog initially so that she didn't look lonely when out walking. After leaving the Home Office – slightly earlier than she had planned – and moving to Fethering full-time, Carole had hated the idea of locals conjecturing about her relationship status or, even worse, pitying her. So, she always looked busy – busy when walking with giving exercise to Gulliver, and busy when in Starbucks with doing *The Times* crossword. She had always been terrified of looking as if she had no purpose in life. In common with many shy people, Carole Seddon worried that other people were far more interested in her behaviour than any of them bothered to be.

She rarely combined a visit to Starbucks with one of her Gulliver walks. Although the management did not object to dogs, some strange puritanism within her didn't like the idea of pets in a venue that served food.

The morning after Jude had visited Rhona Hampton, Carole decided she could justify a Starbucks coffee. It was a Thursday, when *The Times* crossword could be a stinker of a kind that required more than the customary twenty minutes over lunch.

Sure enough, when she sat down with her 'black Americano' and perused the clues, for all the sense they made they might have been written in Serbo-Croat. Some days, she knew, the crossword was like that. The important thing was not to panic. Just calm down, look at the words, break them down into their component parts.

'Well, good morning, Carole. Fancy meeting you here.'

She recognized the voice and looked up to see Adrian Greenford, holding a mug of his customary flat white.

'May I join you, or will I divert your focus from the crossword?'

'Any diversion would be welcomed. It's totally impenetrable today.'

'It'd be totally impenetrable to me any day,' he said as he moved a chair back with his leg and sat opposite her.

Adrian Greenford was a large, red-faced man, dressed that day in a tweed overcoat and grey trilby hat, which he removed to reveal thick hair grizzled like steel wool. He had moved to Fethering some weeks before. Carole was usually resistant to meeting new people, but she had pointed out to him where the eggs were on his first encounter with Fethering's uniquely inefficient supermarket Allinstore. He had then introduced himself, and they'd bumped into each other more than once on the parade or Fethering Beach.

Adrian was one of those people, unlike Carole, who had no problem initiating conversation. He had the bluff, open manner of someone who'd never considered the possibility that people might not want to talk to him. His accent was from the North – he'd told Carole early on in their acquaintance that he and his wife had moved down from Ilkley – and she wondered if that had something to do with it. She shared the common Southern prejudice that people from the North were more outgoing. (In Carole's lexicon, 'outgoing' was not necessarily a compliment. Its shades of meaning moved closer to 'brash' than 'congenial'.)

'So,' she asked, 'how are you settling in?'

'Oh, getting there, getting there,' he replied. 'Place was a bit of a tip when we bought it. Fortunately, a lot of the work was done before we took up residence. The lift's in, which is the main thing, but there's still more to do with ramps and what-have-you.'

'"Ramps"?' Carole echoed.

'Oh, silly me, I hadn't told you. Fact is, my wife Gwyneth is confined to a wheelchair, so there was a lot of sort of adaptation needed to be done to the house.'

'I'm sorry.' Carole curbed the natural instinct to ask what was wrong with her. Though she doubted whether Adrian would have minded answering, it did feel slightly indelicate.

So, she moved the subject on. Though they had met a good few times, the encounters had been brief and a lot of the basic background questions hadn't yet been asked. 'Are you still working, Adrian?'

'No. Retired. You?'

'Retired.' It still caused an obscure pang to admit it. The Home Office had so much defined her life that she had never really found anything to replace it.

'I was in the car business,' Adrian volunteered. 'Salesman for over forty years.'

'Oh?'

Maybe he read some criticism in the monosyllable, because he went on, 'Yes, a car salesman, like they make all the dirty jokes about.'

'I didn't know they made dirty jokes about car salesmen.'

'Oh, come on, surely you must've heard . . .' He looked at her face. 'No, maybe you haven't, Carole.' He sighed, then chuckled. 'Actually, it's quite a relief to meet someone who doesn't immediately go into a routine of car salesman jokes.'

'Do most people you meet do that?'

'Oh yes.'

'Most women?' she asked incredulously.

His big face relaxed into a grin. 'No, I suppose, to be fair, it is mostly the men. Yeah, the men tell the jokes . . . and the women decide which car they're going to buy.'

'Is that how it works?'

'More often than you'd think, yes. Oh, the men come in with all the technical questions about spec and engine capacity and torque measurement and then, generally speaking, they go back home and ask their wives what car they're allowed to buy.'

'"Allowed"?'

'That's usually the way it goes, yes. Let me tell you a story about a man I once dealt with. Potential buyer . . . there was a car he was interested in . . . I had my own showroom back then, and mostly I was a one-man band. Well, I had a couple of boys helped me out part-time . . . and of course a "spivver" . . .'

'Sorry? A what?'

'A "spivver". He tidied up the cars on the forecourt.'

'"Tidied up"?'

'Cleaned them. Kept them polished up. One thing you must never allow in the second-hand car business is a car to have a speck of dust on it. Whatever's going on under the bonnet – and I can assure you I never sold a car that was dodgy under the bonnet, though there's plenty of dealers who do – the bodywork must shine like it's just been cleaned.'

'By the "spivver"?'

'Exactly. You're catching on, Carole. He's got one of the most important jobs. Nobody likes driving away from the showroom in a car that doesn't *gleam*. Of course, within twenty-four hours, their new purchase will be covered with . . .' He checked himself and selected a different word from the one he'd intended. '. . . covered with mud, but that's not the point. When it left my showroom, it *gleamed*.'

Carole reflected on the dusty second-hand offerings she'd seen on the forecourt at Shefford's. They seemed symptomatic of the run-down nature of the business. 'So, presumably,' she said, 'you'd never try to sell a car that'd got damage to the bodywork?'

'No, most of those go to the auctions. That's the place for the wedding rings.'

'Sorry? "Wedding rings"?'

'You call a car a "wedding ring", because you'll never get rid of it.'

'Ah.' Carole was rather enjoying her induction into car dealers' patois. She was also enjoying Adrian's company, though she suspected she wouldn't have it for long. He'd just moved to Fethering, she was one of the first people he'd met. And she was useful to him as a source of local knowledge. Someone as sociable as he was would soon make other friends. Only a matter of time, she reckoned, before Adrian Greenford was the life and soul of the village party, holding court in the Crown and Anchor. Carole had never had any illusions about how interesting she was as a person.

But, at least for the moment, she had his full attention as he continued his narrative. 'Anyway, this guy I'm talking about, he comes in – just off the door, you know – there's a car on the forecourt he's really interested in. When you've done the job as long as I have, you recognize genuine interest when you see it. Do you want to know what make of car it was, Carole?'

'Not really.'

'Didn't think you would. No worries, doesn't change the story. Anyway, in the front window it's got the placard with the price on it. Ten thousand. And that was a fair price. I've always done fair prices. Bit of profit for me, obviously – car's got to wash its face or it's not worth the candle – but otherwise fair price. You try to squeeze too much out of the punters, word soon gets round and you lose your repeat trade. So, yeah, ten thousand is a good price. And I can tell this guy likes it. He checks everything out, he takes it for a test drive . . . he's hooked. So, I get the paperwork ready to close the deal . . . but no, he says he's going home to think about it overnight. And I'm fine with that, because I know he wants it. And a lot of buyers go through that kind of routine. It's a big expense, buying a car, they don't want to rush into it. Don't want to give the impression they're easily persuaded either. No one wants to look like a fool, like they've been done, do they?'

Carole focused on him sharply. Surely he couldn't know about her error with the car insurance, could he? But she was being paranoid. There was nothing sly about the way Adrian continued his narrative.

'So, next day he comes in early, just after I've opened . . . which is good news for me. Means he's made up his mind and can't wait to get the deal sorted. But no, he says, "I do like the car very much and I want to buy it, and I think ten thousand's a reasonable price. But I was talking to my wife about it last night, and she thinks we should only pay nine thousand."

'So I says to him, quick as a flash, "Well, I'd love to sell it to you at that price, but I talked to *my* wife last night and she said we shouldn't accept anything under ten thousand!"'

He roared with laughter, which petered out when he noticed Carole wasn't joining in.

'So did your wife say that?'

'No, of course not. I made it up.'

'Oh.' Carole sounded mystified. She knew she had never been very good at recognizing jokes. 'Did he pay the ten thousand then?'

'Yes,' said Adrian, a little deflated by the failure of his anecdote. It had been a sure-fire laugh-generator on many other occasions. But clearly not on occasions when his audience was Carole Seddon.

'Anyway,' he said, recognizing the moment had come to move the conversation on, 'you've been so helpful to me since we met, recommending local services and so on . . . I wondered if I could pick your brains again . . .?'

'Of course. You're welcome to anything you can find there.'

'Well, it's a matter of garages. I drive a BMW 3 Series Convertible . . .' He looked at her and grinned. 'That probably doesn't mean anything to you, does it?'

'I have heard of BMW,' she ventured cautiously.

'And I was looking for someone round here where I could get it serviced. I mean, obviously I can find the listing for BMW agents, but my car has a . . . slightly unusual service history . . . and I've found you generally get a better job done – and often a cheaper one – at some local garage. Is there anywhere in Fethering?'

So, of course, Carole gave him the details of Shefford's.

Returning to High Tor, she felt quite pleased with herself. She felt she'd made a new friend. While recognizing that it wasn't difficult to strike up a friendship with someone as outgoing as Adrian Greenford, it was still a source of satisfaction.

The fact that he was a man played no part in that satisfaction. Carole Seddon had long before written herself off as a romantic prospect. Indeed, sometimes she found it incongruous to think that she had stayed married to David for so long. Since, following divorce and retirement, she had moved permanently to Fethering, there had been – except for one brief, unlikely involvement with Ted Crisp, landlord of the Crown and Anchor – no special men in her life. And she found that a pleasingly uncomplicated state of affairs.

Unworthy though the thought was, Carole also drew satisfaction from the fact that Adrian was a friend she'd made

without the involvement of Jude. With Carole, jealousy of her
more laid-back neighbour was never far below the surface.

FIVE

As she walked across the gravel driveway to
Troubadours, Jude wasn't convinced she was doing
the right thing. She never felt quite at ease in the
Shorelands Estate. She wasn't sure whether it qualified as
a 'gated community' or not. There were gates at the main
entrance, but she had never seen them closed. That in itself
seemed to say something about the place. Yes, we do have
the exclusivity of a gated community, but we're quite laid-
back about it. Except, in Jude's experience of the residents,
they weren't very laid-back at all.

What they were, all of them, was rich. The Shorelands
Estate, built along the coast to the west of Fethering in the
1950s, was highly sought-after. The residents were people of
the professional classes – solicitors, doctors, dentists, a few
retired diplomats and naval officers. The houses, all huge, were
built in a variety of architectural styles – or it might be more
accurate to say 'based' on a variety of architectural styles.
Black-beamed early Tudor, fancy-bricked Elizabethan, geomet-
rical Georgian, villa-style Victorian were all represented.
Thatched roofs were juxtaposed by Mediterranean terracotta
tiles. Italian pergolas vied with Spanish wrought iron.

Jude always found the ambience claustrophobic. The residents thought they had inherited the earth and all that was
beautiful in it. They were not people who ever doubted their
own entitlement.

She had heard that certainty in the voice of the woman who
had summoned her to the Shorelands Estate earlier in the day.
Natalie Kendrick was the name announced on the phone. She
had heard Jude's services praised by 'people round the village'
(though she didn't name any names) and she would like her
to 'take a look at my son' to see if she could 'do something

for him'. The request was made in the manner of someone
ordering curtain fabric, and Jude had been initially tempted
to refuse it. But her instinct for helping people in trouble –
not to mention her natural curiosity – found her magnetically
drawn to the Shorelands Estate.

Troubadours occupied one of the favoured plots whose
garden gave access on to the beach. Its architectural style was
1930s seaside villa, white-painted with curved walls and metal-
framed windows, reminiscent of an ocean-going liner. On the
gravel drive stood a Land Rover Discovery and another red
car that Jude recognized as a Triumph Tr6. (This familiarity
did not reflect any knowledge of cars, just the fact that she'd
had a brief affair with a man who'd owned one. His pride and
joy. She had very rarely been allowed to drive it – usually
when he'd had too much to drink – but she had enjoyed its
power. The man in question had turned out to be the kind who
was much more interested in cars than he was in women. The
Triumph was flashy, unsubtle and unreliable. Which, given its
owner, had been – she realized later – entirely appropriate.)

The top half of Troubadours' front door was coloured glass,
dark blue for the sea, light blue for the sky, with a white yacht
nearly keeling over at their intersection. Jude rang the bell and
the speed with which it was answered suggested that Natalie
Kendrick had been waiting for her.

She matched exactly the image that her voice on the phone
had conjured up. A thick-set woman probably in her sixties,
she wore sensible black leather pumps, a denim skirt and one
of those fawn padded gilets which imitate the contours of a
woodlouse. The steel-grey hair was parted in the middle and
curled in at the jawline to frame her broad face. Her make-up
was uniform pinkish beige. She was one of those women who
formed the rather unbending spine of England, the affluent
middle class.

'You must be Jude,' she said forcibly. 'Sorry, I didn't get
your surname . . .?'

'Most people just call me "Jude".'

'Right.' Natalie Kendrick's tone suggested the response had
not been entirely satisfactory. 'Anyway, come through to the
sitting room and have some coffee. Hang your coat over there.'

The décor of Troubadours was as predictable as its owner's wardrobe. Beige fitted carpet, custom-made parchment-coloured curtains with a subtle design of foliage, matching pale green velvet sofa and armchairs (all of whose cushions had recently undergone a regimental plumping). One entire wall was windows, curved at the edges, providing, beyond the garden fence, the much-prized sea view.

Coffee was ready on a low table. Tray, cafetière, nice china. Posh, correct.

After the obligatory pleasantries about the weather and recent Fethering events (not many of those), Natalie Kendrick started the proceedings proper by saying, 'As I mentioned on the telephone, it's about my son.'

'Yes.'

'Tom.'

'Yes.'

'He's been going through a difficult time.'

'What kind of "difficult"?'

'The fact is that my husband died three years ago.'

'I'm sorry to hear that.'

'And Tom took it badly.' Somehow there was the implication in her voice that she hadn't taken it as badly as her son had.

'That kind of bereavement can be very difficult for teenagers,' said Jude. 'Everything's difficult for teenagers.'

'Yes.' There was a silence. 'I should perhaps say that Tom wasn't a teenager when his father died.'

'Oh?'

'He's twenty-five now. Twenty-two when Gerald passed.'

'Ah. Well, losing a loved one is difficult at any age.'

'Yes.' For the first time, Natalie Kendrick looked a little flustered. 'I think his father's death definitely made things worse, but Tom's behaviour had always given cause for concern.'

'In what way?'

'He always had trouble, kind of . . . fitting in, I suppose one could say.'

'Fitting in socially, making friends? Has he always been a bit of a loner, is that what you're saying?'

'To an extent, yes. Though he can be quite a gregarious

boy. But . . .' Natalie Kendrick looked the picture of middle-class angst. 'It's the kind of people he likes to mix with that's the problem.'

'Bad company?'

'I'm not sure that they're exactly *bad*, but definitely unsuitable.'

'Ah.' Jude was puzzled. She wasn't sure whether Natalie was building up to some great revelation about her son. Everything she'd said so far sounded pretty imprecise and innocuous. 'Could you explain a bit more about what's wrong with Tom's behaviour?'

'Well, it's just . . . I suppose the problem is that he doesn't really appreciate all the advantages he has.'

'This lovely house . . .' Jude gestured around the room. 'That kind of thing?'

'Yes. More than that, though. Gerald saw to it that the boy went to his own old prep school and public school, and yet Tom didn't seem to realize how fortunate he was. It was almost as if he always wanted something different from life.'

'There's a long history of young people rejecting their parents' values.'

'I am aware of that. But, with Tom . . . I mean, he actually had to leave the public school . . . under something of a cloud. Gerald was mortified. And, since then Tom's been . . . I don't know . . . a drifter. He never settles to things. He's done all kinds of training courses and started jobs. Oh, goodness, there have been so many of them. I mean, it was clear at school that Tom was never going to be university material, so the professions were sort of barred to him. But Gerald and I reconciled ourselves to that.' Something in her tone implied it hadn't necessarily been an easy process.

'So, we – well, I – started looking out more practical forms of training, you know, *apprenticeships*, that sort of thing.' She couldn't keep a slight edge of distaste out of the word. 'We enrolled Tom in computer courses, electrical engineering, carpentry, you name it. He even started learning auto mechanics. But none of them worked out. We considered the hospitality industry. Tom has an easy manner with people, he's well-spoken, we thought he might fit in there. But again, after a few months, for some reason or another, it came to an end. He never seems to stick at anything. Something always goes wrong.'

Jude was beginning to think that she should end the interview. She hadn't exactly been brought to the Shorelands Estate on false pretences. But the 'people round the village' who had recommended her services to Natalie had, not for the first time, misunderstood what she actually did. To the average person, healing was a very vague concept. Though it inevitably encroached on mental distress, the primary focus of Jude's work was dealing with physical ills. And it sounded as though Tom Kendrick, if he required any therapy, needed the help of a psychiatrist rather than a healer.

She spelled this out to Natalie, hoping to make good her escape, but the widow was not diverted so easily from her purpose.

'I think you should at least meet Tom, talk to him. Maybe you will be able to find some common ground.'

Jude shrugged. 'Well, if you like. Since I've actually come here, I'll do that. But I'm not very optimistic that it's going to work.'

'What did *Mummy* say about me?' Tom Kendrick poshed up the word 'Mummy' to give it a satirical edge.

'What do you mean?'

'For example, did she tell you that I was adopted?'

'No. No, she didn't.'

He nodded. He was a tall, large-limbed creature dressed in jogging bottoms and a hoodie, open to reveal a T-shirt advertising the tour of some band Jude had never heard of. He spread himself across a sofa in a posture of indolent ownership.

'No, she tries to avoid telling people if she can. I think that was on Mr Kendrick's orders, actually. He hated telling people I was adopted. Maybe he thought the fact that they couldn't have children was a reflection on his virility. He was very old-fashioned in many ways. Always liked to have his ducks lined up in a row. Didn't like things that didn't fit in.'

'Like you didn't fit in?'

'Oh, well done, yes.' He slowly clapped his hands in dry appreciation.

'Your father had a clear idea of the person who he wanted any son of his to be ... and you didn't fit into that stereotype?'

'You're good,' he said with some surprise. 'Most of the shrinks I've had have taken half a dozen sessions to work that one out.'

'I'm not a shrink.'

'Aren't you?' He didn't sound that interested.

'I'm a healer.'

'Oh God, not another one!'

'What do you mean?'

'Mrs Kendrick brought in another *healer*' – the word was larded with contempt – 'to sort me out. Jeremiah, he called himself. He's local. You know him?'

'We've spoken on the phone. I haven't met him yet.'

'That's a treat in store for you. Then you can get together to chant and throw your special ingredients into the same cauldron.'

Jude had heard enough misinformed slights against her calling not to rise to this one. The lack of reaction didn't seem to bother Tom. He went on, 'I should be flattered, shouldn't I, to be such a rare and incurable case? Having exhausted the resources of the conventional stuff, NHS and private, Mrs Kendrick is turning to alternative medicine. Remarkable, given the views she's expressed on the subject over the years. It'll be Tarot cards next. I must've really got her scared this time.'

'I prefer to think of what I do as complementary medicine rather than alternative medicine.'

'Fine by me. Call it what you want, the fact remains – it's not going to work.'

'Did the man you called Jeremiah help you?'

'No, he was bloody useless. Kept talking about my "aura". And I kept telling him I haven't got a bloody aura!' He looked at Jude pityingly. 'Do you really think that you can heal me?'

'It depends rather on what you think within yourself needs healing.'

'Good answer ... to which my answer would be that I

don't think there's much that needs healing. I think I'm all right as I am.'

'You mean you're happy?'

'Now, come on. I didn't say *that*. No, a lot of the time I'm as miserable as sin, but I don't think that's something that can be *healed*.'

'Are you saying you get depressed?'

'I don't know. A lot of the shrinks have asked me that. Then I ask them what they mean by "being depressed" and they describe it to me . . . and usually I come to the conclusion that . . . no, I'm not depressed. But I am pissed off.'

'And what pisses you off?'

'Everything, pretty much. My situation here. The fact that I'm living on the Shorelands Estate in Fethering with bloody Mrs Kendrick.'

'Can't you move away?'

He shook his head wryly and made that finger-rubbing gesture which is recognized throughout the world to refer to money. 'Can't afford to, can I?'

Jude was increasingly of the view that she was the wrong person to have been called in to sort out Tom Kendrick, but she decided to get a bit more information before she left. 'Your mother said you'd started lots of courses and jobs and none of them had worked out. Why?'

'Because none of them interested me.'

'A lot of people start out doing jobs that don't interest them.'

'Yes, but they *have* to, don't they? I don't.'

'How do you mean?'

'Mrs Kendrick gives me an allowance. So long as that continues, why should I bother?'

'Didn't your father think you should make more of yourself?'

'Maybe. At first. But his idea of me making "more of myself" was doing exactly what he'd done. He'd been Head Boy at prep school, Captain of Cricket at public school, studied Law at university, qualified as a solicitor and settled for a comfortable life of conveyancing, divorce, probate and golf. When it became clear that I wasn't going to go down any of those paths, Mr Kendrick rather lost interest in me.'

'So . . .' asked Jude, 'what do you do all day?'

'Sometimes I go out. Mrs Kendrick has been kind enough to supply me with a car.'

'The Triumph Tr6 outside?'

'That's the one. But I spend most of my time in my bedroom. Got Netflix, Sky Sports, computer games. My needs are simple.'

'What about seeing other people?'

'In my experience, "other people" are very rarely what they're cracked up to be. There are some I get together with in Brighton, but not that often.'

'Girlfriends?'

'Why bother? There are a lot of porn hubs available out there.'

Jude was struck by his negativity and cynicism but was finding it hard to see evidence of mental illness, or indeed of any condition that could benefit from her healing services. She put this to him in as graceful a manner as she could.

Tom grinned triumphantly. 'See? There's nothing wrong with me. I wonder who Mrs Kendrick will turn to next – a witch doctor?'

Jude left the Shorelands Estate that morning with her mind unchanged. Whatever problem Tom Kendrick had, it wasn't one that could be improved by her skills. Indeed, she wondered if he actually did have a problem, except in the eyes of his mother. Tom's lifestyle may not have fitted societal norms, but Jude couldn't see that he was doing much harm to anyone.

SIX

'Don't get old, Carole,' said Bill Shefford. 'It doesn't do you any good.'

'I already am quite old,' she said. She had always felt her age to the last second. Few things annoyed her more than contemporaries saying, 'Oh, I still think like an

eighteen-year-old', or, even worse, 'Age is just a number.'
Who did they think they were fooling?

'Take my word for it, things don't get easier with the passage
of the years.'

'What do you mean?'

It was rare to catch the garage owner in reflective mood.
Rare, in fact, for him to talk to her about anything other than
car-related matters. He looked unhappy, Carole thought, the
heavy features of his freckled face weighed down with gloom.

'Oh, I don't know,' he went on. 'You think you have things
sorted, you think you've got your life worked out, and then
something totally unexpected comes in from left field and you
realize it's all chaos. Things happen at the wrong time. Good
things happen when you're in no position to take advantage
of them. It's all a mess.'

Carole wished she knew the right thing to say. Had it been
Jude sitting on the plastic seat in Shefford's reception area,
she'd have come in with some formula of words that would
have relaxed Bill, maybe encouraged him to further intimacies.
Jude might even have been able to help him, soothe his
despondent mood. Carole knew she didn't have those skills.

She was tempted to ask how long he thought Billy would
take replacing the wiper blades on the Renault, but she knew
that would be copping out. For the first time in their acquaintance, Bill Shefford was opening up to her. She shouldn't reject
the overture.

'Is there,' she asked awkwardly, 'some particular event that's
happened to throw your plans?'

'Life's happened.' He grinned wryly. 'Or perhaps I should
say, death's happened. Not that it's happened yet. But it will.'

Though Carole didn't know how to respond to this gnomic
utterance, fortunately Bill continued without prompting. 'I feel
as if everything's under threat.'

'You mean someone's threatening you?'

'You could say that.' He seemed to realize that they had
strayed outside the normal parameters of their relationship.
'Sorry, you don't want to hear all this.'

'No, I'm interested,' said Carole, something of an under-
statement. Then she came up with a line she had probably

never used before, but which would have made Jude proud of her. 'Sometimes it's better if you talk about things.'

Bill Shefford grinned wryly. 'And sometimes it's better if you keep your trap shut. No point in burdening other people with your problems. Though, on the other hand . . .'

He ground to a halt. Carole quickly posed to herself the what-would-Jude-do-in-these-circumstances question. And came up with the answer: nothing.

Her silence was rewarded by a slight shift in the expression on Bill's face. He fixed his gaze on her. His eyes, she noticed for the first time, were a surprising, almost innocent, blue.

'Sometimes in life,' he began slowly, 'you get into a position where there's nothing you can do that isn't going to hurt someone. There's a decision you have to take and, though you know some people will be very happy with what you've decided, some other people are going to be absolutely devastated.'

'And that's the position you're in at the moment?'

He nodded pensively. 'So, it's a kind of balancing act. A profit-and-loss account, if you like. Is the happiness I'm going to bring to one lot of people worth the pain I'm going to bring to the other lot? Not easy.'

'No,' Carole agreed very softly, afraid to break the fragile atmosphere of his confessional mood.

'And also,' he went on, 'you never know how people are going to react, do you?'

Another scarcely breathed, 'No.'

'If you upset someone, what lengths will they go to . . . to be revenged?'

Silence again. Carole wasn't certain what Bill was referring to, but her mind was teeming with possibilities. Was he talking about the fate of Shefford's Garage, whether he should pass it on to Billy, as everyone expected? Or did he have plans to sell the site? It was a significant lump of real estate in Fethering, with space for a surprising number of new dwellings to be built on it. Yes, there might be an initial problem with organizing change of use, but the local planning authorities were very biddable when there was a prospect of more residential property becoming available.

'And when you have thoughts like that,' he continued finally, 'you can feel very vulnerable . . .'

Yet another pause. Carole hung on his words. Bill Shefford opened his mouth as if for further confidences. But then he changed his mind. Abruptly, he said, 'Anyway, I've got to remove a gearbox', and went through to the workshop.

It seemed to be taking an unconscionably long time for Billy Shefford to change the windscreen wipers on the Renault. Carole felt she should go through to the workshop to chivvy him up, but somehow she couldn't. Her role at Shefford's had always been that of the supplicant, the woman who knew nothing about cars and needed help. Playing that role ruled out the assertiveness she displayed in other areas of her life.

And she did need the new wipers. She'd noticed recently, particularly if driving after dark in the rain, that she couldn't see very well. It was even worse when facing oncoming head-lights. She hoped it wasn't her eyesight, so she'd opted for a change of wiper blades before she made an appointment with the optician.

Was it age catching up with her? Eyes . . . and, of course, the knee. As soon as she thought of it, she felt a twinge and shifted her position on the plastic chair.

As ever, to avoid the ignominy of looking purposeless, she had *The Times* crossword with her, but she couldn't settle to it that morning. Bill Shefford's gloom seemed to have infected her own mood. She looked across at the coffee machine, wondering if it might now contain something drinkable. But, deep down, she knew that such miracles didn't happen.

Suddenly, from the workshop, she heard a heavy metallic thud which coincided with a scream of pain. She rushed through the door from the office.

Billy Shefford and Frankie (whose hair was now jet black) were looking down with horror into the inspection pit, above which a substantial car crouched. Over their shoulders, illu-minated by the pit's sidelights, Carole could see the body of Bill Shefford, crushed by a large metal object.

Billy's next words identified it for her. 'The gearbox,' he said in a voice taut with shock. 'It fell on him. He's dead.'

SEVEN

What happened next was something of a blur for Carole. Billy Shefford didn't want to stay with his father's body. Almost catatonic with shock, he sat silently on the threadbare sofa in the reception area, incapable of any action. It was Frankie who made some calls, presumably summoning an ambulance, though it was obvious that it would be doing the service of a hearse rather than of life-saving transport. Her voice was steady, but unnoticed tears smudged her mascara and made dark runnels down the thick make-up of her face. Carole had the inappropriate thought that, with the jet-black hair, they made her look like a Goth.

As well as the emergency services, Frankie must have made other calls, because fairly soon after, Shannon arrived at the garage. She immediately went to her husband and threw her arms around him. He did not react, still isolated by trauma. Getting no response, Shannon went through to view the crushed body of her father-in-law.

She was absent some ten minutes, then returned. Her eyes were bright with tears. She went to sit on the sagging sofa next to Billy, cradling him like an unresponding baby.

A short while later, Malee entered from the forecourt. Shannon showed no signs of having seen her. Bill Shefford's wife went straight through to Frankie's office. She closed the door, so that Carole could not hear what the two women said to each other. It was a short conversation, then Malee emerged and went into the workshop.

Like her daughter-in-law, she spent some ten minutes with her husband's corpse. Then she came back into the front office and sat on the remaining plastic chair. Nobody said anything.

Still pretending to toy with her crossword, Carole looked covertly sideways at Malee. It was impossible to read what emotions lay behind the impassive, but rather beautiful, Oriental face. Certainly, there were no tears.

Carole now realized there was no role for her to fulfil. In fact, there hadn't been since the accident had happened. With unacknowledged waves to Billy and Frankie, she went out by the front doors. She told herself she didn't go out through the workshop out of respect for the recently deceased, but the real reason was squeamishness. The single glimpse she had caught of Bill Shefford's body in the inspection pit had been quite enough for her.

The Renault was still out the back, exactly where she'd parked it. The new windscreen-wiper blades would have to wait for another day.

'So, he was killed by a falling gearbox?'

'That's what Billy said. And Bill himself told me he had to go and remove a gearbox, so it makes sense.'

'And what might cause a gearbox to fall?'

'Don't look at me, Jude. I know absolutely nothing about mechanics.' The thought struck Carole for the first time that she had now lost her go-to man for such services. Would Billy be as tolerant of her ignorance as his father had been? The thought of not having somewhere to take all her anxieties about the Renault was a worrying one. But she did not voice her anxiety.

'Desperately sad.' Jude sighed. 'From all accounts, Bill had been in a bad way since his first wife died and that's what? Seven years ago. Then he'd just got his life back on track with Malee . . .'

'The "Mail Order Bride",' was Carole's kneejerk interjection.

'I wish you'd stop saying that,' said Jude sharply. 'It's deeply insensitive.'

Carole was used to Jude disagreeing with her, but rarely with such overt criticism. She was subdued by the attack.

They were in an alcove near the welcoming open fire of the Crown and Anchor. Carole had felt disoriented when she returned from Shefford's and had immediately rung Jude. (Going round and knocking on her neighbour's door was not Carole's way. To her, such behaviour had something Northern about it, like the worst excesses of *Coronation Street*.) Jude had suggested lunch at the pub and Carole, who always had to justify everything to herself, thought she deserved it after the traumas of the morning.

It had been only just twelve when they'd arrived at the Crown and Anchor, which felt very odd to Carole. Shock had played tricks with time and she felt sure it must be later than that. Arriving at Shefford's that morning seemed like part of a different lifetime.

They'd both ordered fish and chips, good comfort food for a February lunchtime. (And in Ted Crisp's pub, they knew the fish had been locally sourced.) Each woman had a glass of New Zealand Sauvignon Blanc. Carole had protested she only wanted a small one, but didn't put up much resistance when Jude ordered large. Warmth and company, she found, were diluting the aftershock of the morning's events.

But Jude's rebuke did still sting. Carole couldn't think of a way of apologizing for what she'd said about Malee Shefford, but fortunately Jude, never one to bear grudges, had moved on. 'I wonder how Rhona will react to the news.'

'Rhona?'

'Rhona Hampton. Shannon's mother. I told you I'd been seeing her.'

'Oh yes. For *healing*.' Still disbelief in the word.

'She certainly has it in for Billy Shefford. I haven't heard her express an opinion on his father. But she's sure to have one. Rhona Hampton is one of those women who has an opinion on everything.'

'Did you know Bill well?' asked Carole tentatively, prepared for potential jealousy. She always had the vague fear that Jude would turn out to know Fethering locals better than she did.

'No. I've met him round the village once or twice – in Allinstore, you know . . . But, obviously, not having a car, I've never had any professional dealings with him.'

'No, of course not.' Carole looked pensive. 'I wonder what will happen . . .?'

'What will happen where?'

'With the garage. Apparently, Bill had been talking about retirement recently. And if Billy took it over, he had plans for turning the place into a dealership for one of the big companies.'

'Yes, I'd heard that from Rhona.'

'But what'll happen now?' Carole repeated. 'I wonder whether Bill had got round to making a new will . . . and whether Malee will become the sole beneficiary and inherit everything . . .?'

Jude looked at her friend, wary of another gibe about 'Mail Order Brides'. But there wasn't. Instead, Carole stood up briskly and said, 'I see your glass is empty. Can I get you another?'

'You going to have one?'

'I'll probably just have a coffee.'

'Will you?' Jude looked at Carole again, a small smile lurking round the corner of her mouth. It had the desired effect. Carole said, 'No, I'll have another Sauvignon Blanc.' And they both went up to the bar.

This was partly because Ted Crisp had just appeared from the kitchen. Jude had given their first drinks order to Zosia, his Polish bar manager, but now the landlord was there, in his winter garb of faded sweatshirt and jeans. Maybe in acknowledgement of the cold weather, his beard hadn't been trimmed for a long time. Carole wanted to give him her news. 'Have you heard what's happened up at Shefford's, Ted?'

'That Bill Shefford's had an accident in his inspection pit and died? Yes, I heard about it.'

That was the infuriating thing about Fethering, Carole fumed inwardly. Even if you were the sole witness of an event in the village, it was almost impossible to be the first to tell people. There was a strange telepathy, a kind of bush telegraph, that spread news – particularly bad news – at a speed which most broadband providers could only aspire to. And which regularly frustrated Carole's attempts get there first.

'And,' Ted went on, 'I haven't yet had the lunchtime rush of conspiracy theorists.'

'What do you mean?'

'Oh, come on, Carole. Man dies in suspicious circumstances in Fethering – only a matter of time before half the village have come in here with their ideas of who murdered him.'

'But he wasn't murdered. It was an accident.'

'I'm sure it was. But how many people in Fethering are going to believe that? Anyway, how do you come to be so well informed?'

'Because I was actually at Shefford's when the accident happened.'

'Were you? Respect.' He nodded his head appropriately. 'So, we've got someone in the Crown and Anchor who has an informed opinion about what actually happened in a case of unnatural death. That has to be a first.'

'I don't know why you call it "unnatural death".'

'Having a gearbox fall on your head could hardly be described as "natural", Carole, could it?'

'Well, maybe not.'

'And from what I've heard, there are a few people who could benefit from poor old Bill Shefford being out of the way.'

'What do you mean – from what you've heard?' asked Jude.

'I hear a lot in here. Apart from anything else, Billy Shefford's quite a regular of an evening. And he doesn't keep his opinions to himself. To put it mildly, he's not a fan of his stepmother.'

'Or his mother-in-law?' Jude suggested.

'You're right there. It's difficult to know with Billy, though. I think it's mostly talk, but he's got a short fuse. Quick-tempered. Typical redhead, I suppose. And he doesn't hold his drink well.'

'You mean he gets violent?' asked Carole.

'No, no, he's a harmless drunk. Gets maudlin rather than violent. Sorry for himself. More likely to weep on someone's shoulder than hit them. Sounds off while he drinks his first pint, gets more and more miserable with the second one.'

Carole hadn't thought of it before, but of course Ted Crisp must be in a unique position to classify the kind of drinkers who came through the Crown and Anchor. Over the years he might have built up dossiers on all of them. She hoped he hadn't fitted her drinking behaviour into any category.

The landlord turned a beady eye on her. 'Anyway, Carole, you reckon Bill Shefford is another of your murders?'

'What do you mean – *my* murders. I don't have murders.'

'No? Well, all right, not your own. You share them with Jude.'

He chuckled and Jude joined in. 'Maybe,' she said. 'But I don't think this is one of them. Sounds like a straightforward accident to me.'

'Yeah?' asked Ted. 'Gearboxes are substantial bits of kit. Don't just fall off. If they did, our highways'd be cluttered up with them.'

'Bill did say he was going to *remove* one,' Carole pointed out. 'So, I suppose he loosened the . . . screws or whatever holds the thing in position and then it slipped or . . . I don't know. Do you know how a gearbox is fixed into a car, Ted?'

'Search me. I'm afraid I never was one of those kids who always wanted to know what went on under a car's bonnet. More interested in what went on under a lady's bonnet!' He guffawed, demonstrating once again perhaps why his career as a stand-up comic had been short-lived.

'Tell you, though,' he went on, 'there's a bloke been coming in recently who'd know all about gearbox fixings.'

'Oh?'

'Just moved down here. Ex-car salesman. Got a crippled wife. Adrian something-or-other.'

Carole felt a small pang. She had known that her exclusive friendship with Adrian Greenford wouldn't last long. He'd found his way to the Crown and Anchor without her help.

'He's in most nights,' said Ted. 'I'll ask whether a gearbox is any good as a murder weapon. Oooh, and while I think of new people coming in, there was a bloke the other day asking after you, Jude.'

'Oh?'

Carole another little pang. No doubt this would be another of her neighbour's ex-lovers.

'Some kind of therapist, I think . . . I gave him your number. Hope you don't mind.'

'No, that's fine, Ted. Presumably he gave you a name?'

Ted grinned. 'Jeremiah . . . which is a name and a half, if you ask me.'

'Oh, I have actually had a call from him. We're meeting up next week. Did he say why he wanted to contact me?'

'I didn't really get the details. There were a lot of customers in. But I gathered he wants to set up some clinic here in Fethering, bringing together lots of alternative therapists.'

'I thought it might be something like that. I'm not sure whether that kind of thing would work here.'

There was no surprise that Carole should say, very frostily, 'Nor am I.'

'Well . . .' Ted shrugged. 'When you meet the amazing Jeremiah, Jude, that's what it'll be about. And, incidentally, I wanted to ask—'

But they didn't find out what he wanted to ask, because at that moment the main door of the pub clattered open to admit a man wearing a yellow oilskin over a fuzzy jumper. Barney Poulton, a self-appointed Sage of Fethering, enjoyed propping up the bar of the Crown and Anchor, pontificating on everything and, generally, being one of the banes of Ted Crisp's life.

'Well,' he announced as he entered, 'I hear there's been a murder up at Shefford's Garage.'

And, once again, the Fethering rumour-mill was set in motion.

EIGHT

'I'm no mechanic,' Rhona Hampton declared, 'but I know gearboxes don't detach themselves from the bottom of cars for no reason.'

'What do you mean?' asked Jude, preparing herself for more criticism of the old woman's son-in-law.

'What I mean is that the gearbox must have been fitted with some system of screws or whatever, and the only way of removing it would be by loosening those screws.'

'I agree. And Bill must've been doing just that – loosening the screws – when the gearbox fell on him.'

'You say Bill must've been loosening the screws.'

'Yes, well, he was the one who was working on the car,

wasn't he? He told my neighbour Carole, who was actually at Shefford's when the accident happened – he told her he was going to "remove a gearbox". Which is what he was doing when the thing fell on him.'

'Hm.' Rhona Hampton wheezed. Shortness of breath was becoming an increasing problem for her. 'Bill's been working on cars for over forty years.'

'So?'

'So . . . he wouldn't have to think twice about how to remove a gearbox . . .'

Jude knew full well the direction in which this conversation was going, but she didn't want to say anything that would encourage the old woman's speculations.

'He's not going to make a mistake like that,' Rhona went on. 'You say *he* was loosening the screws. Suppose someone else did the job for him . . .?'

Still, Jude didn't say anything. Though her client was house-bound, she still had a lively network of fellow geriatrics in Fethering. And if she started accusing someone of Bill Shefford's murder, it would be round the village in no time. But surely, however much she disliked Billy, she wasn't about to say he killed his father?

No, she wasn't. Rhona went on, 'And you don't have to look far to work out who sabotaged the gearbox, undid the screws so that, the minute Bill touched the thing, it came crashing down on his head.'

'Who?' asked Jude weakly.

'Well, the new wife, of course. The "Mail Order Bride".' Jude hadn't got the energy to object to the usage. Besides, she had found that attempts to get some understanding of political correctness into her older clients never worked.

Rhona eagerly continued her narrative. 'She traps Bill into marriage. She gets him to change his will in her favour. She—'

'Do you know for a fact that he'd done that – changed his will?'

'I don't need to know it for a fact. I know it happened.' The logic was suspect, but it didn't stop Rhona. 'And then – this is the giveaway, isn't it? – the new Mrs Shefford starts doing evening classes in car maintenance. Now why would someone like her want to know about car maintenance?'

'Since she had married someone who ran a garage, it seems to me quite logical that—'

'No, no, she only needed to get enough mechanical knowledge to work out a way of killing her husband that looks like an accident. Then, while nobody's in the workshop, she loosens the screws and – what do you know? – she inherits the lot.'

'Rhona, I really must say that—'

'There's no two ways about it,' the old woman pronounced definitively, 'Molly or whatever her name is – she murdered Bill Shefford. I've told you before, you can never trust a Chink.'

'This is becoming a habit, Carole,' said Adrian Greenford as he approached her table in Starbucks, flat white in hand. He gestured to the chair opposite. 'May I?'

'Please . . .'

'Thank you. No, we must be careful.'

'Sorry?'

'Meeting in public in a place like Fethering. People will talk.'

'Oh. Yes.' Carole felt herself colouring. She had never had any aptitude for banter, particularly if it came with a hint of the sexual.

'Anyway, how've you been?' he asked.

'Fine.' As ever, she wanted to move on quickly from discussion of herself. 'And you? Getting settled in, are you?'

'Slowly. Everything takes longer than you imagine. Tradesmen don't come when they say they will. And then, of course, with Gwyneth being in the wheelchair, she can't help as much as she'd like to.'

'Oh, of course. I'd forgotten about that. I'm so sorry.'

'Don't worry. She's come to terms with it. Manages to keep pretty cheerful . . . most of the time. I've told her about you, you know, how kind you were to me when I was lost in Allinstore. Gwyneth said you sounded an interesting person. You must meet her.'

'Yes, I'd like to,' Carole lied. Meeting any new people always triggered anxiety in her. And she wasn't sure she wanted to know any more about Adrian's circumstances than the kind of stuff they talked about over coffee. She would like to keep theirs a hermetically sealed, Starbucks-only relationship.

'Incidentally, I gather you had the dubious distinction of witnessing the death that everyone in Fethering is talking about . . .?'

'I didn't actually witness it. I was at the garage when it happened.'

'Very sad.'

'Yes . . . Oh, by the way, did you get to go to Shefford's? When we were last here, you were asking me to recommend a local garage.'

'I did, yes. Met Bill. And his son. Didn't get his name.'

'Billy.'

'Oh, that must've been confusing for them when they lived in the same house. Letters and stuff getting mixed up.'

'I always think it's odd when fathers and sons are given the same name. It seems only to happen right at the top, in the aristocracy where they want to keep family traditions going and, er . . . lower down the social scale, where presumably they haven't the imagination to come up with anything different.' Carole was aware that she had incautiously let her snobbish prejudices show for a moment there. Bit rash, with someone she didn't know well.

But Adrian Greenford's chuckle suggested that he hadn't been offended. Well, he was Northern, so perhaps his standards were more lax. 'I also met Bill's wife. She was there. Stunning-looking woman.'

'Malee.'

'Yes. Did you know – that means "flower" in Thai?'

'Did she tell you that?'

'Good heavens, no. Just something I picked up somewhere.'

'She's Bill's second wife,' Carole explained.

'I pieced that together,' he said, with an edge of irony. 'I hardly imagined that the sylph-like Malee had produced that red-headed hunk Billy. Rather younger than him, for one thing. And call me old-fashioned, but I thought the tradition was that mothers were older than their sons.'

'Yes, of course, Adrian. Silly of me.'

'That's certainly how it happens in the North. But of course it may be different down here.'

To her surprise, Carole found herself grinning. 'No, no, it's the same.'

'Do you believe in the great North/South divide, Carole?'

'Good heavens, no,' she lied. 'People are people every-where.' Which was a most un-Carole-Seddon-like thing to say.

Adrian chuckled, then his face grew more serious. 'Rather a strange feeling, though . . . Bill Shefford. You know, I meet this chap at the garage. Couple of days later, I hear he's dead.'

'I still feel rather shocked by it.'

'Completely understandable, Carole. If you were actually there.'

'Mm.' A silence. Both sipped their coffees. 'Tell me something, Adrian. With your knowledge of cars . . .'

'Yes?'

'How easy is it for a gearbox to come loose like that?'

'Depends very much on the make and model . . . and who's doing the job. With most modern cars it couldn't happen; everything's locked in position within the chassis. And even with older models . . . I mean, needless to say, gearboxes have to be fixed pretty securely in place or our roads'd be covered with ones that'd fallen out. But a skilled mechanic could remove one quite easily. Then again, a skilled mechanic would take precautions to see that he got it out safely.' He grimaced. 'Which is what makes me think there's something odd about what happened to Bill Shefford.'

'What do you mean?' asked Carole, instantly alert.

'Well, I just wonder if he was all right.'

'Sorry?'

'Man in his seventies. Didn't look very fit to me. I wonder if he might have had a seizure, mini-stroke, something like that, which would explain why he allowed the accident to happen.'

'I hadn't thought of that.'

'It would explain why it happened. Still, I suppose that kind of detail will come out at the post mortem.'

'Do you think there'll be a post mortem?'

'Bound to be, with an accident like that.'

'Yes,' Carole agreed thoughtfully. Then, after a pause, 'I don't know if you've been in Fethering long enough to notice that it's a hotbed for gossip . . .?'

'I'd kind of expected that. Small towns and villages are the same all over. It was the same in Ilkley. Gossip can get very cruel and hurtful sometimes.' He was silent for a moment. 'Still, that's what people're like, isn't it?'

'Well, needless to say, everyone in the village has got a theory about Bill Shefford's death.'

'Tell me about it. I was in the Crown and Anchor last night.'

Carole again felt a small, unreasoning pang at the thought of her protégé spreading his wings.

'Nobody could talk about anything else,' Adrian continued.

'Did you contribute?'

He chuckled. 'No, I know my place. New boy. Not yet wise enough in the ways of Fethering to offer an opinion.'

'You soon will be.'

'Oh, I'm sure, yes. There was one bloke in particular who was giving everyone an earful last night.'

'Did you get his name?'

'Barney Poulton.'

'Oh yes,' said Carole wearily.

'Seems to be the local historian, knew everything about the village.'

'Well, he only knows it because he's done his research.'

'What do you mean?'

'Barney Poulton only moved down to Fethering four or five years ago. Previous to that, he commuted every day from Walton-on-Thames to a solicitor's practice in London. His role as the "Sage of Fethering" is one that he completely made up for himself. And a lot of people find it very annoying – particularly Ted Crisp.'

'Sorry? Who?'

'Ted Crisp's the landlord of the Crown and Anchor.'

'Oh, right. The bloke who's mostly beard?'

'Yes.' Carole was annoyed to find herself blushing. For no reason. Her brief relationship with Ted was so long ago

that surely Adrian Greenford couldn't have heard about it.
'So,' she went on, 'what is the Sage of Fethering's view of
Bill Shefford's death?'

'Oh, complete cobblers. Though no more cobblers than
any of the other opinions expressed, actually. Barney Poulton
believes that the car Bill Shefford was working on had
been sabotaged by an undercover organization of White
Supremacists . . .'

'What!'

'. . . who had been deeply offended by his marrying a
woman from Thailand.'

'For heaven's sake!'

'I agree. As I said, though, complete cobblers. Interesting,
though.'

'In what way?'

'The fact that people even entertain the idea of there being
secret White Supremacist cells in West Sussex. It was the same
in Ilkley. A lot of paranoia around these days about that kind
of thing . . . makes you wonder whether there might be some
truth in it.'

'What, you mean truth in Barney Poulton's theory of Bill
Shefford's death?'

'No, truth that there might be White Supremacist cells
around.'

'Nonsense.' There might well be an undercurrent of racism
in Fethering, but nothing so overt as that.

'You're probably right.'

'By the way, you mentioned a make of car, the one that
actually killed Bill. What did you say it was?'

'Oh.' Adrian grinned. 'Friend of mine bought one, showed
it off to me. He said it was built like a tank. I told him it drove
like a tank too. And it did.'

'What was it?'

'Triumph. A Triumph Tr6, to be exact.'

The identity of the vehicle had no resonance for Carole. She
wasn't interested in cars.

The two of them finished their coffees at the same time, so
it seemed logical for Adrian to accompany her along the High

Street. He stopped outside a gate some three houses in. The new metal sign read: Wharfedale. 'This is me.'

'I thought it must be.'

'Oh?'

'Seeing the "For Sale" sign up, and then the "Sold", I worked out that I'd soon have new neighbours.' The casualness with which she said this belied the anxiety with which Carole had anticipated the new ownership. She knew that you could get lucky with neighbours as – she usually conceded – she had with Jude, but there were many other, less congenial, scenarios. So, as ever disturbed by the possibility of change, Carole had covertly watched the comings and goings of potential purchasers, marking them according to her own rigid scale of values.

Given what she regarded as one of the prime locations in the British Isles, Fethering High Street, the property took a surprisingly long time to sell. No doubt behind the delay were many stories of personal heartbreak, of buyer losing the purchasers of their existing houses, of mortgages refused after surveys, of moves being cancelled due to the start of divorce proceedings, and all the other myriad glitches in the English system of house purchase, the least efficient in the known universe.

So, she watched avidly, from behind her front-room curtains, for the tell-tale arrival of estate agents' cars outside what was now called Wharfedale, but had previously been Cozy Cottage. And she rated her prospective new neighbours.

She was worried, on Gulliver's behalf, by the couple who came accompanied by a Rottweiler. Also, the woman's hair was styled in what was locally called a 'Portsmouth facelift', pulled back so tightly into a scrunchy that her eyes were narrowed. Though such coiffeur might be seen on the Downside Estate, it was totally unsuitable for Fethering High Street.

Then there was the family with five children. Cozy Cottage was far too small to accommodate them. Which meant that the children would spill noisily out into the back garden, before taking over the front garden and very soon playing in the streets like pre-war East Enders. The peace of High Tor would be shattered forever.

The less said about the couple who arrived on a motorbike,

the better. The front garden of Cozy Cottage becoming an open-air repair shop, with oily engine parts scattered all over the scuffed lawn . . . it didn't bear thinking of.

Nor was Carole much keener on the pair who came in a Rolls-Royce. Her upbringing had taught her that one of the worst sins in the middle-class lexicon was 'showing off'.

No, in fact she reckoned she'd got off quite lightly with Adrian Greenford.

'Would you like to come in?' he asked, standing at the gate of Wharfedale.

'I beg your pardon?'

'Come and meet Gwyneth.'

'Oh.' It was the last thing she wanted to do. Having just decided that her association with Adrian was going to be a Starbucks-specific one, she didn't want to go back on that so soon. Besides, her right knee was causing her pain and she couldn't wait to rest it in her sitting-room armchair at High Tor.

'I would love you to meet her, and this seems the perfect opportunity . . . that is, if I'm not keeping you from some other commitment . . .?'

Her first instinct was very quickly to invent another commitment. That was one of Carole Seddon's great skills. She had lost count of the number of other commitments she had invented to hide the emptiness of her life.

But she stopped herself. Her second instinct was born of ingrained politeness. To refuse Adrian's offer at that moment would be an act of appalling bad manners. 'No, I'd be delighted to meet Gwyneth,' she lied.

NINE

Adrian's apology for the state of the house seemed unnecessary, even by Carole's exacting standards. True, there were some unopened cardboard boxes in the hall, but otherwise the interior had been furnished and decorated to a very high spec. Of course, in characteristic Fethering style, Carole had known who the old couple who lived there previously *were*, but she hadn't *known* them. One had died and the other gone into a care home, so she expected that the place had been left in something of a state. In fact, she remembered Adrian describing it as 'a bit of a tip'. He and Gwyneth – or, more likely, given her lack of mobility, he – had been busy since they took over ownership. A residual smell of fresh paint confirmed Carole's supposition.

All of the rails and other invalid aids that Adrian had mentioned on their previous meeting at Starbucks were in place. The garden path was levelled asphalt and there was an incline up to the front door. No handrails on the outside but plenty inside, suggesting that, though Gwyneth Greenford could drag her way round the house, all of her outside excursions were in the wheelchair.

As they entered, Adrian called out, 'Gwyn, I've brought someone to meet you,' and ushered Carole into the front sitting room.

The woman sitting in the armchair, with a folded wheelchair beside it, was younger than Carole had expected. She'd had the image of Adrian's crippled wife as being his age, if not older, but Gwyneth Greenford was a good twenty years younger. She was dressed in smart-casual clothes, well-cut dark blue trousers and a silvery silk jumper. Her make-up was expertly done. Whatever her disability might be, there was no visible manifestation of it.

'Oh, hello, Carole,' said Gwyneth.

This instant recognition was a bit of a shock, but when she thought about it, perhaps it wasn't so odd. Adrian had said he'd told his wife about her, and Gwyneth would have had plenty of opportunities to see her walking back and forth along the High Street. The shops on the parade were only yards away from Wharfedale. Instinctively, Carole looked towards the windows. Net curtains, so to see anything outside in detail Gwyneth would have had to peer around the edges. But she wouldn't have been the first person in Fethering to have done that.

'Hello. A pleasure to meet you,' said Carole, in a manner that would have made her parents proud.

'I'd offer to make you coffee, but . . .' Gwyneth spread her hands wide to sum up her helplessness.

'I've just had coffee, thank you. At Starbucks. That's where I met Adrian.'

'Oh.' Gwyneth looked at her husband.

Rather awkwardly, he said, 'Happy coincidence.' Then, swiftly, 'But can I get you anything, my love? A drink or . . .?'

'No, thank you. Ooh, there is something you could do for me, Adrian . . .'

'Yes.'

'There's a parcel in the kitchen that I want to catch the post.'

'Oh, I'm sure there's no rush for that, my love.'

Carole checked her watch. Not yet noon. 'No. You've missed the morning collection at the Post Office. And the afternoon one doesn't go till five thirty.'

'I would like it to catch the post,' said Gwyneth definitively. 'If you don't do it now, Adrian, we'll forget.'

Some invisible marital semaphore must have been exchanged, because he instantly said, 'Very well, my love.'

When he got to the sitting-room door, his wife said, 'Close that. Then Carole and I can get to know everything about each other.'

Carole bridled at the thought. The idea of anyone getting to know everything about her was an appalling one. And, when she came to think of it, a Northern one too. Still, over the years she had managed to frustrate many people's attempts to get near her real self. She didn't think the wheelchair-bound Gwyneth Greenford would prove too much of a challenge.

'So, Carole,' came the opening salvo, 'Adrian tells me you're retired. What did you do during your working life?'

This was easy stuff. A quick résumé of her career at the Home Office (omitting the fact that she was edged out of employment a little earlier than she would have wished). All facts, nothing that came near to being personal.

'And are you married?'

Potentially trickier, but straight, unembroidered answers had worked in the past. 'Divorced,' she said and, to avoid being asked for details, went straight on, 'I have one son, who's married with two daughters.'

It seemed to have worked. No enquiries about the divorce. All Gwyneth said was, 'Adrian and I don't have children.'

Carole did not say anything. 'I'm sorry' was always a risky response. In the past, Carole had been as bored by the rationalizations of couples telling her why they had chosen not to have children as she had by the desolation of those who'd been unable to have them.

She decided to move on to the offensive. 'And you, Gwyneth? Did you use to work?' Fortunately, she stopped herself from adding something on the lines of 'before you got ill'. She didn't want to prompt a litany of ailments.

'I worked in a secretarial capacity for a car dealership in Leeds.'

'Oh? And is that how you came to meet Adrian?'

'Yes.'

A commendably short answer. Maybe Gwyneth was as unwilling to divulge anything personal as she was. That would be very satisfactory, thought Carole, though she still felt a minor pang of unfulfilled nosiness.

Her hostess then went off in another direction, maybe demonstrating some nosiness of her own. 'Your neighbour,' she said, 'the one in the house two away from us . . .'

'Woodside Cottage?'

'Yes.'

'Her name's Jude.'

'I think I'd heard that. Is it true that she works as a healer?'

'Yes,' said Carole, immediately envisioning Gwyneth's demand to be put in contact, followed by Jude's successful treatment of her new client, and a triumphant, but rather embarrassingly sentimental 'Take up thy bed and walk' scenario.

But Gwyneth's next words instantly deleted such images. 'I don't believe in healers,' she said, warming the very cockles of her visitor's heart.

'I agree,' said Carole sleekly. 'There are a lot of charlatans out there.'

'Very true. There were a couple operating where we used to live. I think a lot of them do more harm than good. Raising people's hopes about miracle cures. There ought to be a law against it.'

'You're right. Do you speak from experience, though? I mean, have you tried to get alternative therapy for your' – Carole felt awkward for having strayed on to the subject – 'condition?'

'I certainly have not. It's my view that, if you've got something that the NHS can't deal with, then you should just accept the hand that life has dealt you and get on with it.'

This so exactly reflected Carole's own views that she produced a ringing, 'I do so agree.'

She then realized that she hadn't yet gone through the mandatory local routine for new residents. 'So, Gwyneth,' she asked, 'how're you liking Fethering?'

This was met by a shrug. 'I haven't seen a lot of it. I don't go out much.'

'Oh, I'm sorry. I didn't mean . . .'

'Don't worry. I can go out. Adrian has pushed me along to the parade and the edge of the dunes. It all looks as an English village should. But I prefer to stay indoors.'

'Oh.'

'There's something rather pathetic in being confined to a wheelchair at my age. I don't want to advertise my disability. The last thing I want is people's pity.'

'I can see that.' And Carole could. Though she hoped she never ended up in a comparable situation, she could imagine herself reacting in a similar way. The worst emotion to inspire in others was pity.

'But you like it here?' asked Gwyneth, quite sharply.

'Yes. Well . . . I mean it does have the disadvantages that go with village life . . .'

'Gossip?'

'That kind of thing, yes.'

'Tell me about it. Just the same in Ilkley. Villages, small towns . . . I don't think there's anywhere you can escape gossip. That was one of the reasons we moved.'

'Oh?' asked Carole, instantly alert.

Gwyneth quickly covered up the lapse (if lapse it was).

'Not the main reason, obviously. Adrian was retiring and we both felt like a change of scene. Then we didn't really need all the space we had in the Ilkley house, so downsizing made sense. And moving would be a kind of adventure.'

A strange word to use, Carole thought. Moving from one home you had to negotiate in a wheelchair to another where you would face exactly the same problem. Or maybe the Yorkshire house held memories of a fully functional Gwyneth, who had led a normal life until the illness or accident that had crippled her. Carole was intrigued to know the details, but she didn't think this was the right moment to press for them. She had a feeling she would be seeing a lot more of Gwyneth; time enough to hear the full story of how she had been crippled.

Back at High Tor, Gulliver greeted her with the wild enthusiasm of a dog about to get another walk, and then slunk back to his station by the Aga when it was clear that hope wasn't going to be realized.

Carole stood by the work surface, assembling a cottage-cheese salad for her lunch. She was glad Jude wasn't there watching. Jude's views on the subject of cottage cheese were unprintable.

Then, looking out of the kitchen window, Carole saw something white on the back lawn. A piece of paper. She went out to investigate. Though she left the back door open, Gulliver didn't follow. He knew the limitations of the back garden. Going out that way was never the preface to what he considered a proper walk.

It was a piece of paper. Slid into a transparent envelope to keep the rain off.

It read: 'DON'T THINK YOU'RE OFF THE HOOK YET.'

TEN

Jeremiah was a tall man, probably in his late forties, well muscled with a bulk that could have been intimidating. But it wasn't, because he also carried with him an air of calm. Jude could imagine him being a compelling charismatic preacher. That did not lessen her suspicion of him.

But, as they talked, she found herself warming to Jeremiah. He seemed to anticipate all possible objections. Like her, he had, throughout his career, needed to be ready for accusations of charlatanism and, like her, he had his arguments well marshalled.

Also, Jude could not be unaware, he found her attractive. Over the years, she had got used to this response from men. She never took it too seriously. In most cases, it caused her no more than mild irritation, but with a few her reaction was different. With some, knowing they found her attractive gave her a warm glow. Jeremiah quickly enlisted himself into that small category.

'I know a lot of us in the profession,' he was saying, 'are altruistic about the way we use our gifts. But the fact remains that we all have to make a living, and I've kept thinking of ways to simplify the way our income is generated. We can do a certain amount through the local press, social media can be very effective, but the best way to find new clients is always going to be word of mouth, personal recommendation.'

His views perfectly reflected her own. 'I couldn't agree more,' she said.

'But I was thinking this is still a fairly hit-and-miss approach, particularly for someone like me, just moving to a new area.'

'Remind me – where is it you've come from?'

'Australia most recently. And some years in the States before that.'

'Useful experience?'

'Very definitely. Particularly in the States. California, they're way ahead of this country in their appreciation of alternative therapies. I went to some very good alternative therapy conferences there, learned a lot.'

'Yes, I find conferences very useful. Going to one in a couple of weeks, actually. In Leeds.'

'Oh, what's it called?'

'"Healing Is in the Head".' Jude was glad Carole wasn't there. She could imagine the derision that title would prompt.

'Oh, thanks, I'll check it out online. Anyway, as I'm sure you know, wherever you practise as a healer, it's still a hand-to-mouth existence . . . or is that expression the exclusive property of dentists?'

Jude grinned at the half-joke. 'So . . .' he went on, 'I was wondering whether the situation might be improved by setting up a centre for alternative therapies . . . you know, a permanent venue where people know they can come for a variety of treatments.'

Forewarned by Ted Crisp that this might be the reason Jeremiah wanted to contact her, Jude had had time to form her reactions to the idea. And the main one was scepticism. But she didn't express that straight away. First, find out how much Jeremiah had thought the idea through. 'What, you mean like one of those spas in expensive hotels where they'll cover you with hot stones, drip candle wax on you and walk up and down your back?'

She was proud of the sarcasm in her question – Carole couldn't have done it better – but Jeremiah grinned, as if he'd anticipated her approach. 'You know I don't mean that, Jude. Not somewhere expensive, just somewhere accessible and welcoming. I'm talking about a centre staffed by serious practitioners.'

'Ah, but how do you find them? And how do you check the authenticity of their "seriousness"? As you know, we're talking about a professional area that is not very well policed. Anyone can wake up one morning, decide they're going to be a healer or some other kind of therapist, put a brass plate on their door and wait for the gullible public to stream in.'

'I'm well aware of that. I met my fair share of cowboy therapists in California, believe me. So, I think it's essential that, as well as the unregulated ones, we get some people involved who have recognized qualifications. Quite a lot of GPs working in conventional medicine are open to the idea of alternative therapies, you know. The two are not so far apart. Doctor friend of mine, Bob Rawley, is very keen on the idea of co-operation between them. If the centre I'm trying to get going existed, he'd definitely be doing acupuncture there. And of course, he'd refer patients who he thought might benefit. Complementary medicine, I'm sure that's the future.'

'I don't disagree. But I think you would have to be very careful about who you let in. It only takes one charlatan to unleash a storm of bad publicity and put the image of our profession back a couple of decades.'

'I'm well aware of that. But I think we find the right practitioners by the same method as we currently do clients. Word of mouth, personal recommendation.'

'It could take a long time.'

'Yes, it could. But I'm thinking of the benefits of having a talented group of therapists all in touch with each other, exchanging new ideas, referring clients to each other . . .'

'Hm,' said Jude, hoping it didn't sound too much like one of Carole's 'Hm's. It was rarely that she was as sceptical as her neighbour, but this was fast becoming one of those occasions.

'Look . . .' Jeremiah almost sounded as though he were pleading '. . . I'm suggesting that we start in a small way and slowly build up the reputation of the place, until it becomes a recognized centre of excellence for alternative therapies.'

This plan sounded naïve to Jude, which rather surprised her, because Jeremiah hadn't given her the impression of being a naïve person. 'OK. That's all very fine, but let's face the biggest question: how do you fund such an enterprise?'

'From the therapists who use the facility. When they join, they sign a contract agreeing to pay a percentage of their fees – I don't know, say ten per cent – into a communal pot which pays for the premises.'

Jude grimaced wryly. 'But how do you start? All right, you find your premises . . . and I assume you're talking about renting, not buying . . . and at that point you have no therapists signed up . . . or maybe one or two . . . So, where do you find the first month's rent? Or, come to that, the second month's rent? Or—'

'Yes, all right. I take your point. I'd be prepared to fund the start-up. For a few months.'

'Oh? Do you have a secret supply of money?'

'Why does it have to be a secret supply?'

'Come on, Jeremiah. You're a healer. Very few healers make enough to trouble HM Revenue and Customs.'

'All right.' He coloured. 'I don't have a lot of money, no, but I would be prepared to invest what I do have into a project I believe in.' He looked at her expectantly.

'I don't have much money either, Jeremiah,' she said, and paused before continuing, 'but I'm afraid, if I did, I wouldn't be investing it in your therapy centre . . . if that's what you were asking me to do?'

'Well, not exactly . . . I mean, obviously, I would have been delighted if you had wanted to contribute, but I wanted to see you more to use you as a sounding board, to see if you think the project is a good idea.'

Jude twisted her lips. 'It may be a good idea, Jeremiah. That I don't know. But it's not a good idea for *me*.'

'Oh?'

'For me, healing is a very private interaction between me and the client. I need privacy to build up the required concentration. Though I am sure that working in a place where there were lots of other therapists with whom to exchange ideas would be very pleasant socially, I don't think it would help me to do my job. I think it might actually make it more difficult.'

'Oh well.' Jeremiah grinned, a reassuring grin. 'Fair enough. I thought it was worth asking.'

'Always worth asking anything.'

'Yes.'

'So how long have you been in the area, since you came back from Australia?'

'Getting on for six months now.'

'In Fethering?' If so, Jude was surprised she hadn't seen him around.

'No Fedborough.' He referred to the larger town, some six miles upstream on the River Fether.

'And are you liking it here?'

'Yes, very pleasant area. I should think it's nicer in the summer.'

'Certainly is.'

'We just caught the end of the last one, then a rather wet autumn.'

'Tell me about it.' Jude had registered the 'we'. Suggested he had a partner, a wife maybe. She felt the smallest of pangs.

'Anyway, I seem to have built up quite a respectable list of clients. Some over in Worthing, and as far away as Portsmouth to the West.'

Jude nodded. 'That's more or less my catchment area too.'

'No lack of ailments on the Costa Geriatrica,' said Jeremiah with a grin.

It was the first thing he'd said wrong. Nothing overt, but just a slight hint of callousness, as though the clients existed for his benefit more than because they were people needing help.

There was a silence, then Jeremiah said, 'I heard in the Crown and Anchor that your neighbour was actually present at Shefford's Garage when that awful accident happened.'

'Yes. Carole Seddon. She was.'

'Terrible business.'

'Mm. Did you know Bill Shefford?'

Jeremiah shrugged. 'I'd met him. Been in there to get petrol, that's all. Did you?'

Jude shook her head. 'Like you, I'd met him. You don't have to be long in a place like Fethering before you know everyone. But I only knew Bill for a polite nod and a "Good morning".'

'Your friend Carole knew him better?'

'A bit. She always went to Shefford's when there was something wrong with her precious Renault. I don't have a car.'

'Ah.' Another silence. 'Needless to say, a lot of speculation about the death last time I was in the Crown and Anchor.'

'You don't surprise me. Everyone convinced it was murder

– and the perpetrator identified as everyone from Cain the
Killer of Abel to Russian undercover agents?'

'That's about right.' He grinned. 'Does your neighbour have
a view?'

'On whether Bill Shefford was murdered?'

'Mm.'

'What makes you think she might?'

'The landlord at the Crown and Anchor . . .'

'Ted Crisp.'

'Ah. I didn't get his name.'

'He mentioned that you two had a bit of a reputation locally
as amateur sleuths.'

'Did he?' said Jude drily. 'Well, it is the view of my neigh-
bourly Miss Marple that Bill Shefford's death was an accident.
Sorry to disappoint you.'

'I'll survive.' Jeremiah's smile suggested he wasn't that
disappointed. 'Oh, incidentally . . .'

'Mm?'

'I wondered if you had been contacted by a woman called
Natalie Kendrick . . .?'

'Why?' Jude was instantly and instinctively alert. If
Jeremiah was going to ask her about her healing work, he
would find her surprisingly circumspect. She had high standards about protecting the confidentiality of her clients.

'Just that she consulted me about helping her son. Boy –
well, man – called Tom. I wondered whether she might have
contacted you too.'

'Why should she have done?' asked Jude, still cagey.

'Because I was no bloody use to her. Or to him.'

Jude considered her moral position. Technically, Tom
Kendrick was not one of her clients. She had talked to him,
at his mother's request, and didn't reckon she could help with
whatever was wrong with him . . . if indeed there was anything
wrong with him. Jeremiah, who had gone further into the
therapeutic process, didn't seem to be constrained by any
confidentiality worries. So, there was no reason why she should
discuss Tom with him.

'I was rather in the same boat,' she said. 'Whatever he did
need, I don't think it was my kind of healing.'

'Or mine. I thought he needed – to use a technical psycho-therapeutic term – a kick up the backside.' Jude giggled. 'He seemed to me to be just a layabout – and nothing was going to change that situation, until his mother cuts off the very generous allowance she was giving him.'

'I came to the same conclusion.' A pause. 'But why did you suddenly bring him up, Jeremiah?'

'Because of his connection to Shefford's.'

'I didn't know Tom Kendrick had a connection with Shefford's.'

'Oh yes. Amongst the many courses and things that his mother set up for him, he did spend some time working at the garage.'

'I didn't know that.'

'Just on a casual basis. I think the idea was that, if it went well, it might be formalized into some kind of apprenticeship. But, needless to say, because it involved Tom Kendrick, it didn't go well.'

'Did he learn anything?'

'A bit of basic mechanics, I gather. Bill Shefford had been very generous in taking him on. The Kendricks' family cars were always serviced at the garage and she persuaded him to give the boy a chance.'

'I can imagine.' Jude had encountered too many women of Natalie Kendrick's type to have any doubts about their powers of persuasion.

'But, of course, Tom screwed up. After a couple of months, he was asked to leave.'

'What for? Anything specific?'

'I don't think so. Just general inefficiency, turning up late, skiving, you name it. The customary behaviour of a layabout with a private income.'

'Ah.'

'Apparently, Bill Shefford was very upset by Tom's behaviour. He'd bent over backwards to give the boy a chance, and he'd had his generosity thrown back in his face. According to what I heard, Bill Shefford was the mildest of men, never lost his temper, never even raised his voice. But when he finally sacked Tom Kendrick, there was a great shouting match.'

'Really?'

'Yes. In front of all the staff and customers, I gather.'

'Who told you this?'

'Tom himself. Well, his version was slightly different from
what I've just told you. In his version, he'd done nothing
wrong. He was just trying to do his job, but Bill Shefford kept
picking on him. Tom was still clearly very angry.'

'Was he?'

'Yes. There was a lot of bad blood there.'

ELEVEN

'I don't know about cars,' said Carole, with some pride.
There were some areas of life where she felt it was permissible – even admirable – to admit ignorance.

'But you must have noticed,' Jude insisted. 'You saw the
car that was over the inspection pit, didn't you?'

'Yes, of course I did.'

'Then what make was it?'

'As I told you, I don't know about cars. But someone told
me' – she was still circumspect about mentioning Adrian to
Jude – 'that it was a Triumph.'

'What kind of Triumph?'

'I can't remember.'

Jude sighed with exasperation, sat back in their Crown and
Anchor alcove and produced her mobile from a pocket. Her
fingers flew over the tiny keyboard.

Carole watched with suspicion and a tinge of jealousy. She
distrusted the fluency with which some people conducted their
whole lives on mobile phones. Rather in the way her neighbour
was doing at that moment. It couldn't be healthy. It was part
of some Faustian pact. What would happen if all of the mobile
networks in the world ceased to function simultaneously?
Carole Seddon was big on apocalypse scenarios.

But then she reminded herself she must be on top of
the video-making capacity of her new phone before her

granddaughters arrived in March. All that WhatsAppery, she must get it right.

Jude found what she was looking for and thrust the screen towards her friend. 'There! That is a Triumph Tr6. Was the car whose gearbox killed Bill Shefford a Triumph Tr6?'

'It does look quite like it,' Carole admitted. But she wasn't going to give up her treasured ignorance so easily. 'But I don't really know about cars.'

'You have made that point,' said Jude, with a rare flash of asperity. 'At least I presume you can tell me what colour it was.'

'Red,' said Carole penitently. It was so unusual for her neighbour to snap at her that she felt a little subdued.

'Then,' said Jude triumphantly, 'I'm pretty sure I know who owns it. And I also think that we may have to reconsider our conclusion about Bill Shefford's death being an accident.'

Excitement sparkled in the pale blue eyes behind Carole's rimless glasses. 'What do you mean?' she asked breathlessly.

So, Jude told her about seeing Tom Kendrick's Triumph Tr6 at Troubadours. This obviously led to questions from her neighbour about what had taken her to the Shorelands Estate. And her answer prompted the entirely predictable response of a sniff and 'Oh, one of your *healing* things.'

'As it turned out, it wasn't "one of my healing things".'

'Oh?'

'I didn't reckon he needed healing. Tom Kendrick is just a lazy young man who has his mother entirely wrapped around his little finger.'

'Really?'

'And if I was doing any healing there, I certainly wouldn't be talking about him.'

'Oh yes, of course. Your precious client confidentiality.'

Jude sighed. It was sometimes very tiring engaging in conversation with Carole. But she did relay what she'd heard from Jeremiah about the bad blood between the young man and Bill Shefford. 'I don't know,' she concluded. 'May be simple coincidence, but if one was looking for evidence of foul play . . .'

'I'm definitely looking for evidence of foul play,' said Carole, completely hooked. She didn't realize until that moment how disappointed she had been by the accident theory of Bill Shefford's death.

'I think the first thing we need to find out,' said Jude, 'is whether the murder method is feasible.'

'How do you mean?'

'Would it be possible to sabotage a Triumph Tr6 in such a way that the gearbox could fall down on top of someone inspecting it? I suppose I could look online. There's always plenty of stuff about vehicle mechanics, but I'm not sure that kind of information would be easy to track down. Or indeed whether I'd understand it if I did track it down.'

'Don't worry,' said Carole, once again feeling ascendancy. 'I can find that out.'

'How? As you keep saying, you know nothing about cars.'

'No,' Carole agreed complacently, 'but I know a man who does.'

'I know there's nothing one can say about foreigners that isn't classified as racist these days.' The pontificating voice came, unsurprisingly, from Barney Poulton. He was incapable of being in the Crown and Anchor without pontificating, and how long he'd been at it could usually be judged by the thickness of the glaze on Ted Crisp's eyes. Customers like Barney Poulton were one of the hazards of a landlord's life. Every pub had at least one person who fitted the brief and the Crown and Anchor had quite a few. Unfortunately, that night Barney was the only one of them present, which ruled out the possibility of someone else with an equally large ego interrupting his monologue.

'But,' he went on, 'if you aren't allowed to mention people's nationality, then how are you going to pass any comment? Whether that comment be commendation or criticism?'

Carole looked across at the bar, then turned back, eyebrows raised in annoyance. 'He does go on, doesn't he? I'm glad to say he hardly knows me, so I think I'm safe from having to hear his opinions.'

'Don't you believe it. Barney talks so loudly no one can avoid his opinions.' Jude swallowed down the last of her Sauvignon Blanc and moved to rise from the alcove. 'I think we need to get another drink.'

'But if you go up to get them,' Carole hissed fiercely, 'he's bound to buttonhole you.'

'Exactly. But haven't you noticed who he's with?'

Carole gaze strayed back to the bar. 'Ah. I see what you mean.'

She too downed the remains of her glass and followed Jude across the room.

By now, Barney Poulton was naming names. 'If there were to be any official investigation, I think there's no question that Malee Shefford would be the first person the police would want to interview.'

'With you there,' said Frankie, whose presence it was that had hurried Jude to the bar with a second order of Sauvignon Blanc. Frankie was drinking something that looked like Coca-Cola but smelt strongly of rum. On the counter in front of Barney Poulton was the half-empty pint glass which was such an essential prop for his self-appointed role.

Jude saw the relief in Ted Crisp's eyes at their approach. 'Two more of the usual, is it?' he asked her, glad to have something else to do, apart from listening to the Sage of Fethering.

Jude greeted Barney and Frankie warmly. Though she didn't know either of them well, she didn't suffer from her neighbour's hang-ups about the difference between 'people who you know who they are' and 'people who you've been introduced to'. Carole had had many dealings with Frankie at Shefford's, so she reckoned that was the equivalent to being introduced. She had, however, previously managed to avoid one-to-one conversation with Barney, so her greeting to him was appropriately awkward and aloof.

'We were talking,' he explained, as though his voice hadn't been loud enough to fill the entire bar, 'about the recent death of the much-lamented Bill Shefford.' He made it sound as though he'd been cruelly deprived of the company of an old friend. Whereas, if they had once or twice had a discussion about repairs to his car, that was the extent of their acquaintance-ship. But to his mind, Barney Poulton's fiefdom covered all of Fethering.

'And I was expressing the opinion that his wife – now widow – Malee could not be excluded from any discussion on the subject. Of course, I don't say that because she's of foreign extraction.'

How often in Fethering, Jude wondered, had she heard people say the exact opposite of what they felt?

'I say it because, when there is an incident of a suspicious death, one's first question has to be: "*Cui bono?*"' Barney seemed to decide that using Latin tags did not chime appro-priately with his image as a salt-of-the-earth Fethering local, so went on to explain, 'Who benefits from the crime? And when a married man is murdered, the most likely beneficiary is his wife.'

'That may be the case,' said Jude, not liking the assump-tions that were being so quickly made. 'But that doesn't mean that the wife is guilty of any crime. We don't even know that we're talking about a murder, do we?' This was in spite of what she had just said to Carole. Jude didn't want to encourage further gyrations of the Fethering rumour-mill.

'I think we are,' said Frankie firmly.

'Talking about a murder?' asked Carole.

'Yes. I've worked with Bill Shefford for more than twenty years. One thing he could never be accused of is carelessness, particularly when it came to Health and Safety. All right, he was old-fashioned in some ways. He preferred working in the inspection pit to using the hydraulic lift, which caused a few arguments with Billy. Billy wanted to fill in the pit and buy a second hydraulic lift, one with a higher spec that they could use to do MOTs. God knows how many times I've heard him say, "There's money in Ministry of Transport testing, Dad." Billy always had new ideas for updating the facilities, but Bill always found ways of avoiding further investment. He wasn't mean, mind you, just cautious.'

'Probably more cautious after he'd married Malee,' Barney contributed.

'What do you mean?' asked Jude.

'She would have discouraged him from spending, so that there was more for her to inherit.'

'You don't know that.'

'Oh, I do, Jude, I do. You see, the thing is with "Mail Order Brides" . . .' He launched into another subject on which he apparently had encyclopedic knowledge. 'When UK men marry them, they don't realize that they're not just taking on the upkeep of the bride herself, it's her whole family. Just you watch – as soon as probate's sorted, Malee'll be back in wherever-she-came-from, introducing hordes of relations to a much better lifestyle than they have any right to expect.'

Jude pursed her lips. She wasn't enjoying this xenophobic diatribe. She looked across for support from Carole, but her neighbour's expression was ambivalent. Carole could be distressingly blinkered about certain subjects. Jude decided not to protest further, just see if any useful information emerged from the conversation.

'Yes, I've heard that,' said Frankie. 'Moment I saw Malee for the first time, the expression came into my head. "Gold-digger". She was only ever after Bill's money. He was a sitting duck, really, once she'd got her claws into him. Bill was so lonely after Valerie died. Cancer it was. Her last couple of years weren't much fun. I wouldn't have been surprised if Bill had married soon after that, you know, kind of on the rebound after Valerie's death. There were plenty of women in Fethering who would have been glad to have him. Didn't talk a lot, but he was a really kind man, not many like him around.'

Jude wondered for a moment whether Frankie herself might have been one of the women who 'would have been glad to have him'. She spoke with definite fondness. Maybe that might explain her violent antipathy to Malee. Or maybe Jude was reading too much into the situation.

'Which means, of course,' Frankie continued, 'that he was a pushover for someone like Malee. It's very sad, really. I thought she would at least have waited till he died naturally to get his money. But no, she was too greedy.'

Jude couldn't keep quiet any longer. 'Do you know for a fact,' she asked, 'that Malee was going to inherit everything?'

'Well, of course she was,' said Frankie. 'Otherwise what would have been the point of killing him?'

The argument was totally illogical, but Jude didn't take issue with it. She just said, 'Quite often, when older men remarry, they draw up wills which make provisions for their existing family as well as their new wife. And from what you say about Bill's kindness, that sounds just the kind of thing he might have done.'

'He might have wanted to do that,' said Frankie stubbornly. 'He might have intended to do that. But Malee would've persuaded him against the idea. She'd have made sure he named her as his sole beneficiary.'

'Do you actually *know* that?' asked Jude again. 'Did he tell you what was in his will?'

'He didn't have to tell me.' Logic was clearly not a strong point with Frankie. 'But I know what I know. And I know Malee killed Bill.'

'You may remember,' said Carole, after a brief silence, 'that I was actually in the garage when he died . . .'

'Course I remember,' said Frankie. 'Billy was sorting out your wipers, right?'

'Yes. And I was just wondering . . . how Malee could have had anything to do with Bill Shefford's death. I mean, she wasn't there, was she? She arrived some time after he died.'

'I know that.' Frankie's tone was almost pitying. 'But she didn't have to be there when he got killed. In fact, she couldn't have been, because Billy would have seen if she got up to anything dodgy. Certainly, if she went down into the inspection pit. No, she'd sabotaged the Triumph Tr6 earlier, loosened the gearbox screws so that it came down on Bill as soon as he touched it.'

'When could she have done that?' asked Jude.

'Night before,' Frankie pronounced with great certainty. 'She'd got keys to the garage, see? Bill'd given her a set, though why she needed them I don't know.'

'It wouldn't be unusual for a wife to have a set of keys to her husband's place of work.'

'You reckon?' Frankie almost sneered at Jude's suggestion.

'I think she made him give them to her, so that she could snoop around. I think she looked through the files on my computer.'

'Why would she do that?'

'Doing evening classes in book-keeping, wasn't she? I'm sure she got into my files, looking for some mistakes or dodgy doings, she may even have planted stuff on the computer. Incriminating stuff, so that Bill would be left with no alternative but to give me the elbow. That Malee definitely had her eyes on my job.'

Jude was surprised by the level of paranoia in the woman's words. 'If she did do that,' she said, 'and I think it's very unlikely that she did, that still doesn't mean she committed murder.'

'It meant she had the opportunity to commit murder,' Frankie insisted. 'And she wasn't just doing evening classes in book-keeping. Car maintenance as well. Why would she be doing that if it wasn't to find out how to sabotage a car?'

Frankie's logic was becoming ridiculous. Jude objected, 'There are lots of reasons why she'd want to do car maintenance. If you marry someone who owns a garage, then it's quite normal that you'd be interested in his work. You might even want to be able to help him out at times.'

'Oh yes?' Frankie very definitely took this the wrong way. 'So, you're saying she was after Billy's job as well as mine, are you?'

'I am certainly not saying that. I'm just saying that if anyone's going to go around making public accusations of murder, they should be pretty sure of their ground.'

'I am sure of my ground,' Frankie countered. 'I'd put money on the fact that Malee tampered with the gearbox fixing on the Triumph Tr6. She wanted to kill Bill and she wanted it to look like an accident.'

Carole joined the conversation. 'If that was the case, and if there was any suspicion of foul play, then surely the police would investigate?'

'Haven't heard anything from the police,' said Frankie. 'And the garage had recently had an HSE inspection and—'

'HSE?' Jude queried.

'Health and Safety Executive. Everything was up to date there. Then, obviously the ambulance people came. They seemed to think it was an accident. And there was a doctor.'

'Who was the doctor?' asked Carole. 'One from the Fethering Surgery?' She knew who they were, though she hadn't been introduced to all of them.

'I didn't recognize him,' said Frankie. 'But apparently Bill'd been to see him quite recently. So, there was no problem about signing the death certificate.'

'That sounds rather odd,' said Carole. 'Surely the body would have been taken by ambulance to the hospital and—?'

Frankie, however, didn't want her narrative interrupted. 'It was all above board, from that point of view. And, as I say, Health and Safety too. But it was made to look like an accident, so the police didn't need to be involved. I haven't heard a dicky bird from them.'

'Maybe,' Barney Poulton insinuated, 'the police will only take action if someone tells them there's a suspicion of foul play . . .?'

'Some public-spirited local resident?'

Unaware of the sarcasm in Jude's voice, the Sage of Fethering replied, 'Yes. Exactly.'

He and Frankie looked at each other intently. Jude reckoned they were assessing which one of them would take on the role of 'public-spirited local resident'.

But Frankie hadn't yet finished with her condemnation. She looked firmly at Jude, as if she had already won Carole round to her way of thinking. 'And do you know why I'm sure that Malee arranged Bill's death?'

'No. And I would like to know, because all the arguments you've come up with so far have been—'

'I'll tell you why I know,' Frankie interrupted.

'Why?'

'Because, when she saw Bill's body in the workshop . . . she didn't shed a single tear.'

TWELVE

'Who is this?'
Since she'd phoned Adrian's mobile, she'd
expected him to answer it, so was surprised to
hear a female voice.

'Oh, is that Gwyneth?'

'Yes.'

'It's Carole Seddon.'

Was there a slight hesitation before the 'Hello'?

'I wanted to speak to Adrian.'

'Yes, of course. Well, he's not here at the moment. He's
doing some shopping for me. And left his phone at home
again. I'm afraid Adrian has never really bonded properly with
mobiles.'

'They still don't feel entirely natural to our generation, do
they?'

'Certainly not to his generation.' There was a sharpness in
the response. Gwyneth's disability had blinded Carole to the
age difference, but when she thought about it, she realized
that Adrian could be as much as fifteen years older than his
wife.

'Well, if you could just ask him to give me a call . . .'

'Of course.'

'On the landline would be best. He's got both my numbers.'

'I'm sure he has,' said Gwyneth.

Which, after she'd finished the call, Carole thought was
rather an odd thing to say.

Adrian didn't get back to her that day, and her going to
Starbucks the following morning had, she told herself firmly,
nothing to do with the possibility of seeing him. She was,
nonetheless, quite gratified when he did appear at the table
where, only a few minutes before, she'd sat down with her
Americano.

'Hello, stranger,' he said. 'May I join you?'

'Of course,' she said. 'And less of the "Hello, stranger". You're the one who's been proving elusive.'

His brow furrowed in puzzlement. 'What do you mean?'

'I mean you didn't return my call.'

'What call?'

'Oh? Didn't Gwyneth tell you?'

'You rang Gwyneth? On the landline?'

'No, I rang your mobile and she answered it.'

'Ah,' he said. And then, as if it wasn't important, 'Oh well, she must just have forgotten to pass on the message.' But Carole got the feeling it might have been important to him.

'Anyway,' she said, 'the reason I wanted to talk to you was to pick your brains about matters car-related.'

'I might be able to help there. What is it?'

'You remember telling me that the car that killed Bill Shefford was a Triumph?'

'Yes. A Tr6.'

'I wondered how easy it would be to remove the gearbox.'

'Ah. So what they say is true.'

'I'm sorry. I don't know what you're talking about.'

Adrian grinned. 'I'm discovering there's lots of gossip in a place like Fethering.'

'Tell me about it.'

'Just like Ilkley, in fact.'

'And what gossip have you heard about me?' asked Carole defensively.

'That you and your friend Jude have a bit of a reputation locally as amateur sleuths.'

'Oh. Well, as you know, most gossip is ill-informed and inaccurate.'

'Hm.' He gave her a look of amused scepticism. 'So, it's just out of general curiosity that you want to know how easy it is to sabotage the gearbox of a Triumph Tr6?'

'Yes.'

'From your well-known fascination with 1970s Triumphs?'

'Of course.'

Her defiant response made Adrian's grin spread wider.

Carole looked away, or she would have found herself grinning too. Which would have been most unlike her.

'All right,' said Adrian. 'How technical do you want me to be?'

'As untechnical as possible, please. Pretend you're talking to someone who knows nothing about cars and has no interest in them.'

'"Pretend"?' he echoed, and Carole could suppress her grin no longer. He continued, 'All right, here we go. There would be slight differences according to the spec of the vehicle but I'm assuming you're not particularly interested in that.'

'You assume correctly.'

'OK. One end of the gearbox is bolted on to the engine with six or maybe eight heavy-duty bolts. If those had all been removed, there's no way someone in an inspection pit or under the vehicle on a ramp wouldn't notice. So, I think it's unlikely that would be the way it was done . . . if we are acting on the assumption that someone had sabotaged the car.'

'For the purposes of this exercise, we are.'

'Right. Now at the other end of the gearbox, which would probably have an overdrive attached, it's held in place by two heavy-duty bolts, which also go through a rubber plate which acts as a kind of shock-absorber. Removing it under normal circumstances would involve setting up some harness or a small hydraulic lift to take the weight, undoing those two bolts, as well as the ones attaching it to the engine, and lowering the gearbox from the vehicle.

'But, if I was thinking like a cold-blooded killer, wanting to booby-trap the car and use it as a murder weapon . . .'

'Please think like that, Adrian.'

'Very well. Then I would loosen one of those bolts – the ones that go through the rubber plate – completely, and the other one almost completely, so that the minute it's touched, this whole heavy mass of metal comes crashing down on whoever is unfortunate enough to be underneath it.' Adrian looked at her with a lopsided grin. 'Is that too technical for you, Carole?'

'No,' she breathed with satisfaction. 'It's perfect. And would it require a lot of strength or advanced mechanical knowledge to do that?'

'Not a lot of strength if you've got the right tools, which a garage like Shefford's definitely would have. And not much advanced mechanical knowledge. Anyone who'd spent time working around cars would know how to do it.'

'Ah.'

'That was a very profound, sleuth-like "Ah", Carole.'

'I wouldn't say that.'

'I would. So now, I suppose, from my minimal reading of crime fiction, you make a list of suspects who might have had the technical expertise . . . and opportunity . . . to sabotage the Triumph Tr6 on top of Bill Shefford's inspection pit.'

Carole felt a little taken aback. She was used to having such conversations with Jude and not with anyone else. And yet the idea of discussing the 'case' (as she found herself thinking of it) with Adrian Greenford was not without its attraction. Like her friendship with him, it felt exciting and slightly daring.

'Well, I suppose we could do that,' she conceded. 'You start.'

'I don't know much about the opportunity side of it, who would have access to the garage, who'd have keys, so that they could set up the booby-trap when the premises were closed . . . which I guess is the way it would have been done.'

'If it were done,' Carole cautioned him.

'If it were done,' he repeated piously. 'My guide in these matters is what I hear in the Crown and Anchor.'

'A very unreliable source of information.'

'I'm sure it is, Carole.'

'In fact, for the engendering of fake news, Barney Poulton and his cronies could give both the Russian and American intelligence services a run for their money.'

'Right.' Adrian grinned. 'From this very unreliable source then, two names emerge. One is obviously Billy Shefford. It's common knowledge that he had had conflicts in the past with his father over the future of the garage. He sounded off in public on many occasions about how the old man was dragging his feet about making the changes that were needed in the business. Also – and this was from Barney Poulton, so is doubly suspect – there is a suggestion that Billy wanted his father out of the way before he had time to change his will in favour of his second wife.'

'And do we know that was the case? What the provisions of his former will were and whether he had yet changed it?'

'No, of course we don't. As I said, the source of this suggestion is Barney Poulton, none of whose theories are ever backed up by the thinnest wisp of research. But let me say that, though there is a kind of logic that fingers Billy as chief suspect, it is not a suggestion that finds much support in the Crown and Anchor.'

'Why not?'

'Because Billy's a regular there. All the other regulars are his mates. And they're not going to grass up one of their own. Besides, and this is a slightly more compelling argument, he's been so public about his criticism of his father. Everyone in the Crown and Anchor has heard him whingeing on about the old boy. The general view is that someone planning to commit murder would be a little less vocal about the shortcomings of his proposed victim.'

'That's quite a good point. And the Crown and Anchor's second suspect?' Carole knew the answer, but she didn't want to volunteer more names until she had heard in full the wisdom of the pub's regulars.

'Well, of course, it's the new wife, isn't it? Malee.'

'Have you met her?'

'Yes, I have. Yes. Very briefly.' He seemed about to say more but changed his mind. 'I'm afraid with someone like her, you don't see the attitudes of an English country village at their best. From what I've observed, Fethering seems to distrust newcomers, even if they've only come from as far away as Fedborough. So, when you've got someone all the way from Thailand . . . and that someone marries a well-loved local, whose first wife Valerie was very popular in the village . . . Did you ever meet her, by the way, Carole?'

'No. I think she must have died before I started living down here full-time.'

'Ah. Well, anyway, in the Crown and Anchor's favourite scenario, Bill Shefford had changed his will, leaving everything to Malee.'

'This is based on the same amount of knowledge of the facts as supported the thesis that he hadn't yet changed it?'

'Identical. And that meant, of course, that she had the perfect motive to kill her husband . . . so that she would inherit everything . . . which was the only reason she married him in the first place.'

'I see.'

'But making Malee the prime suspect is not just racism and distrust of the outsider, though there's plenty of that. The clincher for the Crown and Anchor Major Incident Team is that she had apparently been taking evening classes in car maintenance. I don't know if that's true . . .?'

'It is.'

'Ah. Case proved then. Why would Malee want to take evening classes in car maintenance except to learn how to sabotage a Triumph Tr6 so that its gearbox falls and kills her husband?'

'I can think of a good few reasons.'

'So can I. But we are perhaps a little less blinkered than the Crown and Anchor Major Incident Team. So far as they're concerned, Malee did it and should be instantly arrested. End of story.'

'Hm.' Carole took a sip of her Americano. It had gone cold during their recent conversation. 'And the Crown and Anchor aren't considering any other suspects?'

'Should they be? You probably know more than I do. You were actually at Shefford's when it happened. Anyone else you'd put in the frame?'

'Well . . . Don't let this go any further . . .' Even as she said the words, she knew it was a pretty stupid thing to say in Fethering. But that didn't stop her continuing. 'Billy's wife Shannon is very protective of him. She'd have the same motives as he would, I suppose, protecting their inheritance. And the garage had been the centre of his life right through their marriage, so she might have been round there enough to have picked up some mechanical knowledge.'

'Possible,' said Adrian.

'Then again, Frankie – you know, in the office at Shefford's – she must have absorbed quite a lot of mechanical knowhow over the years she's been there.'

'Mm.'

'And Jude sort of wondered whether Frankie might have been holding a candle for Bill for some years and had her nose put out of joint when he married someone else.'

'Does she have any proof for that?'

'No. But Jude's a pretty shrewd judge of people.' Carole wondered why she was praising her neighbour to Adrian. And then again, why it should worry her that she was praising her neighbour to Adrian?

'So . . .' he asked, 'is that it? Or are there any other suspects?'

Carole was about to mention Tom Kendrick, the fact that he was the owner of the Triumph Tr6 and the fact that there had been bad blood between him and Bill Shefford.

But, for some reason, she didn't.

When, later that day, Carole went through the potential suspects with Jude, she didn't mention that it was the second time she had done the exercise. A slight element of mystery about her relationship with Adrian Greenford still seemed appropriate. This time she did, however, add Tom Kendrick's name to the list.

'Yes,' said Jude thoughtfully. 'I must somehow arrange to talk to him again.'

'What – so you've changed your mind about his condition, have you? Think he does need healing, after all?'

'No.' Jude sounded almost testy. 'I wouldn't do that.' She hadn't the energy to go through the arguments again with Carole about her attitudes to healing. 'I'll find a way to contact him. And I'd better do it before the weekend.'

'Oh?'

'I'm going up to Leeds on Friday morning.'

Carole would rather have pretended not to be interested, but she couldn't stop herself from asking, 'What for?'

'A conference.'

'And what's it called?' asked Carole with exaggerated patience.

'"Healing Is in the Head",' Jude admitted.

No words could have been as expressive as Carole's snort of derision. It was exactly the reaction Jude had imagined when she mentioned the conference to Jeremiah. Then, from Carole, 'You're not speaking at it, are you?'

'No. A couple of my friends are.'

'Oh?'

'Karen and Chrissie. Their subject is: "Healing in the LGBT Community".'

'Oh, my goodness. Does that mean they're . . .?'

'A lesbian couple, yes.'

'Oh.'

Jude giggled. 'Just like a lot of people in Fethering think we are.'

Carole's face was a study in unamusement.

THIRTEEN

'He's upstairs. I'll get him.'

As the line went quiet, Jude wondered whether Natalie Kendrick always answered the phone when it rang in Troubadours. Was she acting as some kind of gate-keeper for Tom? Then she rationalized that he probably had a mobile on which he conducted all his personal calls. But she was still intrigued by who held the power in that particular mother/son relationship.

She hadn't completely prepared the approach she would take when he came on the phone. She certainly wouldn't pretend her call had anything to do with healing, as Carole had suggested. When it came to her work, Jude had a strict code of ethics. Healing was not to be messed with.

'Hi,' Tom said languorously. 'Changed your mind, have you? Think you can heal my non-existent ailment?'

'No.' She decided, as she often did, that the truth might be as good an approach as any other. 'I wanted to talk to you about what happened with your car.'

'Ah. The Triumph Tr6. Or, as it is better known currently around Fethering, "The Murder Weapon".'

'That's the one.'

'And why do you want to talk to me about it? Presumably because of that? Because of its role in Bill Shefford's death?'

'Yes.'

'Well, at least you're honest.'

'What do you mean by that?'

'I mean lots of the Fethering gossips are muttering behind their hands about me. At least you're coming straight out and saying that you think I had something to do with topping the poor bugger.'

'I'm not saying that.'

'No? Then why do you want to talk to me about it?'

'Straightforward curiosity. A desire to find out what actually happened.'

'Honest again. But give me one good reason why I should talk to you?'

Jude was thrown by the question and improvised madly. 'Erm, because you are getting sick of . . . as you say, "lots of the Fethering gossips muttering behind their hands" about you. Because, if we found out what actually *did* happen that morning at the garage, they'd all get off your back.'

'Hm. Yes, I do share your curiosity about that. Incidentally, were you the one who was in Shefford's when it happened?'

'No.'

'Oh, it must've been your partner then. People always talk about you two together.'

Jude grinned inwardly, remembering their recent conversation. 'It was Carole Seddon, my neighbour.'

'Right. So, she might actually have some hard facts to contribute to the discussion?'

'I'm sure she will have.'

'OK then. I don't mind seeing the two of you together.'

'Good.' Jude was delighted. And she knew Carole would be too. 'Where do you want to meet? We'd be happy to come to your place.'

'No.'

'The Crown and Anchor?'

'God, no. That'd be like poking a stick straight into the gossips' wasps' nest. No, we need to meet somewhere more private.'

Tom Kendrick's idea of 'somewhere more private' was a pub in The Lanes in Brighton. Carole complained about this, because parking in the city was always difficult. But when they got there, the setting was so markedly different from anything in Fethering that they understood his logic.

One of the big differences was the average age of the clientele. Though in the tourist season the Crown and Anchor would see a good few holidaymaking families, in the winter it was mostly locals, which meant retired people. Brighton had a much younger demographic. In the pub were thin young men challenging the weather in skimpy T-shirts, young women in clashing clothes and hair colours that extended the range of nature's palette. And nobody seemed to be untattooed.

The pub was full for early afternoon, but the clientele didn't seem to be just relaxing. There was an air of busyness. Laptops and tablets were much in evidence. Their loud chatter and wild gesticulations had an earnestness about them. They seemed to be discussing work projects, almost definitely arts-related.

The place wasn't 'private' in the sense of 'empty' or 'quiet', but the very noisiness provided its own security. Everyone there was far too interested in their own conversations to bother eavesdropping on anyone else's. Events in Fethering felt a very long way away.

The venue made Carole acutely uncomfortable. She was sure everyone was looking at her, though in fact nobody bothered. Jude, never much concerned what other people thought of her, was completely at her ease as she pressed her way through the crowd to greet Tom.

He had taken off his hoodie, revealing long arms which had their own share of tattoos. He was in conversation with a couple of other T-shirted young men, one with blond dreadlocks, but they scuttled away at his visitors' arrival.

Tom had the remaining third of a pint of Guinness on the

table in front of him. He agreed to Jude's suggestion of 'another of the same?' Carole opted for a sparkling mineral water 'because of the driving'.

She thought the conversation wouldn't start until Jude returned with the drinks, but Tom Kendrick ploughed straight in. 'You were in Shefford's when Bill Shefford was killed?'

'Yes.'

'Did you actually see what happened?'

'No. I was in the reception area. He was in the workshop.'

'Hm. You know it was my car he was working on?'

'I didn't realize at the time, but I know now.'

'Which some people in Fethering seem to think makes it likely that I set up the booby-trap deliberately to kill him.'

'I'm not one of those people.'

'Glad to hear it.'

Carole was glad too that, at that moment, Jude rejoined them. Tom thanked her politely for the drink. His upbringing by Natalie Kendrick had taught him the basics of civilized behaviour.

He then looked shrewdly at each of them in turn. 'OK, the reason we're meeting is because it's possible you two might be able to stop the gossip going around Fethering about me.'

'The best way we can do that,' said Jude, 'is by finding out what actually *did* cause Bill Shefford's death; whether it was just an accident or whether foul play was involved.' She met Tom's gaze. He looked away. 'Can I ask why you're so concerned about Fethering gossip?'

'Why shouldn't I be?'

'It's just, on very brief acquaintance, you don't come across to me as the kind of person who cares much what other people think of him.'

He grinned with self-recognition. 'You may be right. But, if the police were to get involved in investigating what happened . . . well, I wouldn't be so keen on that.'

Jude didn't ask why. She got the feeling drugs might be in the background, some possible previous charges against him, but that was his business.

His words had attracted Carole's interest, though. 'Have the police been involved?' she asked. 'Have any of them been in touch with you?'

Tom shook his head. 'Though if Fethering gossip continues at its current rate, that situation might change. And since it was my car what dunit . . . well, I think I have reason to be a tad anxious.'

'Maybe,' said Jude.

'Look,' said Carole baldly, 'there is something that's come up which I think we can't avoid mentioning.'

'Oh? And what's that?'

'We know that you worked at Shefford's for a while.'

'I'm not denying it. Another of Mrs Kendrick's attempts to make me a "useful member of society". Another failure, needless to say.'

'And we did hear that you had a serious falling-out with Bill Shefford.'

That caught him on the raw. 'Who did you hear that from?'

Jude answered. Once again, she saw no reason not to tell the truth. 'I heard it from the other healer who your mother tried to set up for you.'

'Oh. Jeremiah.' He drenched the word in contempt. 'Yes, he was as useless as the rest of the profession . . . if "profession" isn't too generous a term for that bunch of charlatans.'

Jude knew he was being deliberately offensive but did not rise to the insult. Nor did she look at Carole, who was quite capable of nodding agreement to the sentiment.

'Oh yes,' Tom went on. 'I suppose all you lot get together, don't you, to spread nasty stories about your patients?'

Though this insinuation offended her even more, still Jude kept her own counsel. So, it was Carole who asked, 'But what Jeremiah said was true? You did have a falling-out with Bill Shefford?'

'"Falling-out"?' He grimaced as he echoed the word. 'I think that's putting it a bit strong. He wanted me to work hard for him in a business in which I pretty soon realized I had no interest. So, we didn't see eye to eye. I wouldn't put it any worse than that. Our disagreement certainly didn't bother me enough for me to set up a booby-trap to kill the guy.'

'But you would have had the mechanical skills to do it if you'd wanted to?' asked Carole sharply.

'Maybe. But as I say, I'm far too lazy to bother with an elaborate scheme like that. Sorry to disappoint you but, beneath my lackadaisical exterior, there isn't a rampant psychopath desperate to commit further atrocities.'

Not for the first time, Jude was struck how articulate Tom Kendrick was. He might have disappointed his father by the route he'd taken thereafter, but his public-school education had not been wasted. 'Presumably,' she said, 'while you were working at Shefford's, you did get a chance to see what was going on there?'

'How do you mean?'

'You would have been able to get a feeling of the kind of tensions within the business . . . or within the family who ran the business?'

'Oh, I see what you're doing.' He let out a grunt of laughter. 'If it's not me in the frame, who do I think the murderer might have been?'

'Yes, all right. If that's the way you want to see it.'

'And I would like to say,' Carole pointed out, 'that in crime books and television programmes, a time-honoured method of diverting suspicion from oneself is finding the proof of who actually did commit the murder.'

'I get it.' Tom took a long swallow of Guinness. 'All right, the way I saw things, from my position as a humble and deeply unwilling apprentice, was that there was obviously tension between Bill and Billy about the way they wanted the business to develop. Billy had big plans and his old man kept dragging his feet about getting them implemented. I reckon Billy had reconciled himself to waiting till his dad retired before he could turn Shefford's into what he wanted it to be.'

'And did you ever hear Bill talking about retirement?' asked Carole. 'Did he say when it was likely to happen?'

'He didn't specify a date.'

'And when was it you were working there?'

'Last autumn. October, November, I suppose.'

'Really? Because apparently he used never to talk about retirement.'

'Well, he definitely did when I was there. Kept on about it, in fact.'

'And when he did retire,' asked Jude, 'was he planning to stay round the Fethering area?'

'Now that's interesting.' Tom took a swig of Guinness. 'I got the impression staying local had been his intention. You know, being around Billy's family, the grandchildren. But I think his plans may have been changing.'

'Oh?'

'He did more than once talk about the idea of retiring to Thailand.'

'With Malee?'

'Obviously.'

Carole followed the logic. 'Which might have meant that he would sell up the premises in Fethering and take the proceeds out to Thailand . . .'

'Maybe. He didn't say that, but I guess it's possible.'

'Did you see much of Malee?' asked Jude. 'You know, while you were working there?'

'She came in quite a bit, actually. Very interested in everything that was going on. She appeared to be intrigued by the mechanics of cars, just in the way that I wasn't.'

'So, she would have had the skills . . .?' Carole hazarded.

'Oh yes, she could have loosened the fixings of a gearbox, no problem.'

'When she came into the garage, after Bill Shefford's death, Shannon, Billy's wife, was there. She didn't even acknowledge Malee.'

'That's no surprise. Shannon took against her even more than Billy did. She was very, like, protective of him.'

'Yes, I got that impression,' said Jude, her mind freewheeling to questions about how far the protective instinct would extend, when her husband – and his inheritance – were under threat. Like her mother, Shannon Shefford was a very strong personality, who might be capable of anything when the security of her family was at stake.

'Incidentally,' asked Carole, suddenly changing the subject, 'what happened to your car? The Triumph Tr6. I mean, presumably it's been examined . . . you know, for forensic evidence?'

'Why would it be examined if the police haven't been involved?'

'What?' Carole looked curious. 'So where is it now? Still at Shefford's?'

'No, it's parked up the road here.'

'You drove to Brighton in it?'

'Of course I did. I haven't got another car.'

'So, when did you get it back?' asked Jude.

'Day after the accident. That's when they said I'd get it back. Serviced, valeted, looked like new.'

'"Valeted"?'

'Yes, inside and out. Looks brilliant.' Carole wondered who'd done that. From the look of the second-hand cars on its forecourt, Shefford's did not run to a 'spivver'.

'And any evidence that might have shown it had been booby-trapped was effectively removed?' she asked.

'Guess so.'

Although she knew the answer, Carole still asked, 'Who did the service?'

'Obviously . . . Billy Shefford.'

FOURTEEN

'Well, Shannon wasn't going to get any cooperation out of *her*, was she?'

Jude was once again exercising her palliative-care skills at Waggoners. And Rhona Hampton was once again denigrating Bill Shefford's widow.

'So, what, you say Shannon asked if she could look through the house for a will?'

'Yes, well, that's reasonable, isn't it, Jude? She'd been on to Bill's solicitor and they had no record of him having made a will. He never was that good with paperwork. Never much bothered about paperwork, come to that. He relied on Frankie to keep the business on the right side of the law. You know, she looked after the invoices . . . and the tax . . . and the Health and Safety Executive stuff . . .

'So, anyway, Shannon rang Malee and asked if she'd found some informal hand-written will round the house . . . because they can be legal, you know. There was a case recently where some old bloke had scribbled his will on a McDonald's paper napkin and that was legal, so it can happen. And Malee had said she'd looked round the house and found nothing. So, then Shannon asked if she could have a look. And Malee said, "No." Just like that. I mean, what kind of a way is that to treat your . . . what? Stepdaughter-in-law?'

'She's within her rights. It is her house.'

'But is it, Jude? Is it? Surely that depends on the will. And if there isn't a will, then who knows whose house it is?'

'I think you'll find, Rhona, that under British law, if a woman is legally married at the time of her husband's death, and he's intestate – in other words, he hasn't made a will – then she inherits all of his estate.'

'That's not fair, is it?'

'It may not be fair, but it's the law. And I take it Malee was legally married to Bill?'

Rhona grimaced. 'Yes. Only a registry office thing. Back last February. I was invited, but there was no way I was going. Shannon and Billy went. They said it felt more like a funeral to this side of the family.'

'And what about her side of the family? Were any of Malee's relatives there?'

'No.'

'Must've been fun for her,' said Jude wryly, trying not to visualize the grisly details of the occasion. Malee's progress in becoming part of the Shefford family cannot have been easy, and having no backup from her own side could only have made things worse.

'No,' Rhona went on, 'her people were no doubt back in Thailand, busy on their calculators, working out how much money they'd get when Bill kicked the bucket.'

Jude knew there was no point in saying anything. Rhona

Hampton was not about to change such entrenched attitudes at this advanced stage of her life.

'Shannon'll try again,' Rhona went on. 'Not easily put off, my daughter. She'll be back at that house and she'll get in, even if she has to break in. She'll find the will that Bill drew up before he met his "Mail Order Bride".'

'Could you just move on to your other side?' asked Jude. She helped ease the frail body on the bed. There now seemed to be only a thin layer of skin over the old woman's bones. Jude's healing efforts were helping with the pain, but Rhona was also on a lot of prescription medication. She was not much longer for this life, but she was still capable of great malignancy where Malee Shefford was concerned.

In shifting her client's position, Jude dislodged a pile of A4 sheets from the bedside table. With Rhona settled, she bent to pick them up.

'Oh, those are copies of Bill's death certificate,' said the old woman. 'I told Shannon they were going to need lots of them. You can never have too many. I remember when my Roy passed, I couldn't believe how much paperwork there was, and how many people needed to see a copy of the death certificate. So Shannon got lots of spares from the registrar.'

Jude was only half-listening. She had seen something on the death certificate that intrigued her.

'Shannon's a tough woman,' said Jude. 'No question. She's incredibly protective of Billy. I get the impression he's quite a weak character, maybe grew up too much in the shadow of his father. But Shannon's more than ready to fight his battles for him.'

'How far do you reckon she'd go?' asked Carole. They were sitting over coffee in the High Tor kitchen. Gulliver snuffled in his dog dreams by the Aga.

'As far as killing the father? Is that what you're asking?'

'Well, it's a thought.'

'I don't know. I can see her squaring up to Malee, no problem, but I somehow get the impression she was fond of her father-in-law.'

'Maybe. Fondness hasn't been allowed to stop a great many murderers.' Carole took a sip of coffee. 'Do you believe in the existence of this earlier will that Rhona mentioned?'

Jude shrugged. 'No idea.'

'Of course,' said Carole, 'in all of our speculation about the case' – she now had no problem with using the word – 'there's one person we haven't talked to . . .'

'I was thinking just the same.' Jude took out her mobile. 'Thinking it to such an extent that I put her number into my phone.' She pressed a couple of buttons.

'We are talking about Malee, aren't we?'

Jude nodded and listened to her phone for a few seconds. 'Still the answering machine. Still with Bill Shefford's voice on it.'

'Still?' asked Carole. 'What, you mean you've tried Malee's number before?'

'A few times.'

Carole couldn't stop herself from saying, 'Without telling me?'

She took a note of the number and, after Jude had left, tried calling it herself. She didn't know why she thought the outcome would be any different. And it wasn't. She too got the answering machine message from the late Bill Shefford.

But, unlike Jude, she left a message, identifying herself, reminding Malee that she had been at Shefford's when her husband had died, and asking the widow to call her.

'Hello, Jude. It's Jeremiah.'

'Oh, hi.' His voice down the phone was pleasantly warming. 'How're you doing?'

'Fine, thank you.'

'I'm glad you called.'

'Thank you.' He didn't pick up the implication in her words. Never mind, she would bide her time before she asked the questions she wanted to. 'Let me tell you, Jude, I'm still thinking that setting up my centre for alternative therapies in Fethering is a good idea.'

'Best of luck with it.'

'I gather from your tone that you're no more keen than you were when we last discussed it.'

'You gather correctly.'

'Ah, well. When it's a huge success, written up in medical journals around the world, the go-to destination for A-list addicts, and you come begging on your hands and knees to be allowed space within it, I will be prepared to be generous.'

Jude giggled. 'In the completely impossible event of that scenario arising, I will still probably not accept your generosity.'

'It's a good offer.'

'Appreciated as such. Anyway, to what do I owe the honour ⁿ this call?'

'ⁱ iust gather that you've seen Tom Kendrick again.'

'How uo you know that?'

'I had a call from his mother. Trying to persuade me to have another go at treating him. And she said you'd seen him.'

'I hope she didn't imply that I'd changed my mind about whether I could help him.'

'No. To be fair to her, she didn't.'

'And did she persuade you that you could do something for him?'

'I did say I'd go and meet up with him again, see if I could get anywhere.'

'But, if you couldn't the first time . . .'

'He kind of intrigues me. An unusual case. I think it's worth having another go.'

'OK.'

'I was just interested in why *you* saw him again . . . and whether it had anything to do with what I told you about his relationship with the late Bill Shefford.'

Another of those occasions when there was no point in Jude telling anything but the truth. 'Yes, that was why I saw him.'

'And?'

'Do you mean: "*And* did he immediately confess to having sabotaged the Triumph Tr6 with a view to killing the boss he'd fallen out with?"'

'I wasn't expecting quite as much as that. I am interested in what he said, though.'

'But, Jeremiah, you still wondered whether he might have pointed the finger of suspicion towards anyone else? Am I on the right track?'

He sighed. 'Not far off. I'm afraid I'm just as caught up in murderous speculation as the rest of Fethering.'

'OK. I'll tell you what I found out from Tom but, in return, there's something I want you to tell me.'

'Sounds fine. If slightly mysterious.' A thoughtful silence. Then, 'All right. You said there was something you wanted to ask me . . .?'

'Yes. The first time you talked about your plans for the therapy centre, you mentioned a doctor friend of yours called "Bob Rawley" . . .'

'I may well have done. I've had a lot of dealings with him over the years. An NHS doctor who really believes in complementary medicine. He's a great advocate of acupuncture.'

'And his full name's "Robert Rawley"?'

'Yes.' A chuckle. 'Fortunately, he can pronounce his Rs. Why are you asking me about him?'

'Because Robert Rawley is the name of the doctor who signed Bill Shefford's death certificate.'

'Oh.' The news did not seem to be particularly unexpected to Jeremiah. 'Well, he's a qualified doctor, living in the area. Is that so surprising?'

'He's not one of the doctors in the Fethering Surgery. Most people locally are registered there.'

'So? Bill Shefford was registered somewhere else.' Again, he made it sound like it wasn't a big deal.

'Jeremiah . . .' – Jude pieced her thoughts together slowly – 'the fact that Dr Rawley signed the death certificate suggests he had been treating Bill Shefford . . .'

'Not necessarily.'

'Well, he must've seen Bill within a fortnight of his death. Otherwise, surely there would have had to be a post mortem?'

'Perhaps.'

'In fact, I'm quite surprised there doesn't seem to have been a post mortem.'

'Do we know there hasn't been?'

'Frankie at the garage said there hadn't been. But I'd have thought, in the case of an accidental death like that . . .'

'Pretty straightforward. There's not much doubt about what killed him.'

'No.' Jude was about to tell Jeremiah about the speed with which Billy Shefford had completed the Triumph Tr6's service and had the vehicle valeted. But something stopped her. 'Your friend Dr Rawley didn't mention to you whether he'd been treating Bill Shefford, did he?'

'No, of course he didn't. Come on, Jude, you know the code of confidentiality that medical practitioners have about their patients.'

Oh yes, she knew all about that.

FIFTEEN

'So,' asked Carole, 'are you suggesting that Billy Shefford was involved with this Dr Rawley in some kind of cover-up?'

'I don't really know what I'm suggesting,' said Jude. 'It just seems odd to me. How did Bill Shefford get in touch with Dr Rawley? Because, do you remember, when we were with Frankie in the Crown and Anchor, she said Bill had been seeing the doctor who signed the death certificate? She didn't mention the name, though.'

'Yes, I remember.'

'I mean, you, with your Home Office background, do you know what happens after an accidental death? Does there have to be a police investigation or an inquest?'

'I don't think there *has* to be,' said Carole judiciously. She wanted to maintain her professional image, but in fact this wasn't an area in which she had any specialized knowledge. 'There might be an investigation from the Health and Safety Executive . . . though Frankie said they'd recently had an inspection from them.' Finally, she confessed, 'I really don't know.'

'Hm. Well, if there's anything you can find out while I'm away . . .'

'Away?' Carole echoed, puzzled.

'I told you, I'm going to Leeds in the morning.'

'Oh yes, of course,' said Carole. 'To your lesbian conference.'

When Carole came downstairs the following morning, the Friday, there was a piece of paper on the High Tor doormat. The message read: 'DON'T THINK YOU'RE SAFE, YOU BITCH!'

Her first instinct was to ring Jude. Then she remembered her neighbour had already left on her trip up North. It wasn't worth calling her on the mobile. Carole didn't want to sound needy.

But she did want to find out who was responsible for this campaign of harassment against her. Though, perhaps surprisingly, her stronger imperative was to find out the truth about Bill Shefford's death.

So, with her neighbour away, she thought she might do a little investigation on her own. The idea of presenting Jude with new information – or even, dare she hope, a solution – on her return was rather appealing.

Somehow, Jude's absence increased Carole's confidence. She started her research online, at the laptop in the spare room, seeking out alternative therapists in the local area. The number of listings surprised her. All kinds of services were offered in Fethering and Fedborough, extending to Worthing and Brighton to the east, Chichester and Portsmouth to the west. She went through them meticulously. Some were individual practitioners, others attached to therapy centres. It took a long time to find the name she was looking for.

Having found it, she was faced by a dilemma. Jude, of course, had a strict code of ethics in medical matters, but Carole was not restricted by such considerations. And, in spite of the level of success she'd seen her neighbour achieve with various clients, her own level of scepticism about the whole healing business remained high. Though she would never have dreamt of lying to anyone in the NHS, she thought alternative therapists were fair game.

So, she rang through to the Magic of Therapy Centre in Smalting and made an appointment that afternoon to see Dr Robert Rawley.

'So, it's the right knee, is it, Mrs Seddon?' he asked.

The Magic of Therapy Centre operated from a converted – and presumably deconsecrated – church. Smalting was a small seaside village to the west of Fethering. Its residents thought they were socially superior to Fethering's. Mind you, Fethering's thought they were socially superior to Smalting's. But Smalting didn't have a cultural excrescence like the former 'council housing' of the Downside Estate within its boundaries, so its residents reckoned that settled the argument.

Dr Rawley was a long thin man, dressed in a black shirt and black jeans. Carole preferred her doctors in sports jackets like the ones at Fethering Surgery. But then what could you expect from practitioners who embraced alternative as well as traditional medicine?

Carole had not yet taken her knee to the proper doctors. She knew what would have happened if she'd gone to Fethering Surgery. She almost definitely wouldn't have secured an appointment with the one doctor she trusted there – and whom she used to think of as '*her* doctor'. She would instead have been fobbed off with some eleven-year-old trainee, who would have looked at her knee and referred her to St Giles's Hospital in Clincham for an X-ray. Whose inconclusive results would take weeks to arrive back at the surgery. And when they did arrive, the surgery would forget to tell her and she'd have to ring them.

She wasn't expecting anything very different going private at the Magic of Therapy Centre, but she reckoned the expense was justified as part of her investigation in Bill Shefford's death.

With a view to having her knee examined, she had worn a skirt rather than trousers and, in spite of the cold weather, no tights. Just socks under her sensible shoes. She didn't relish the indignity of having to take any clothes off.

Once she had confirmed that the right knee was the one causing her problems, Dr Rawley asked her to stand and move her foot in various directions, first with shoes on, then without. She had to tell him which positions caused pain, and he noted the result on an iPad.

Next, as requested, she lay down on the treatment couch while he felt and manipulated the offending limb, once again noting the movements which made her wince.

He asked her to get off the couch and take a chair. Then he announced, 'I would say it is definitely arthritis.'

This was far from good news for Carole. The word 'arthritis' carried such heavy connotations of age and decrepitude. She didn't think she was old enough to be even distantly associated with the condition.

'Presumably,' she said, 'your diagnosis could be confirmed by an X-ray?'

'It could be,' Dr Rawley agreed, 'though it would be a waste of effort to take one.'

'Why?'

'Because, as you observed, it would only confirm what I've just told you. What is causing the pain in your knee is arthritis.'

'I'm sure, if I'd gone to my usual doctor, he would have recommended having an X-ray taken.' She didn't mention the unlikelihood of her actually getting an appointment with her usual doctor.

Dr Rawley shrugged. 'That would have been his decision, and I am not about to question the decision of a fellow practitioner. It is my view, however, that an X-ray is unnecessary and a waste of expensive resources.'

'Oh.'

'And, incidentally, I think I would be justified in asking, if you so favour the methods of your usual doctor, why aren't you at their surgery consulting them? Why have you come to see me?'

This was too direct a question, and one for which Carole had not really prepared an answer. She replied evasively, 'I've had your services recommended to me.'

'That's good. From a satisfied customer?'

To say 'No' would sound stupid. She wished she hadn't started off down this particular track. So, she said, 'Yes.'

'May I ask who?'

She was stuck with it now. 'Bill Shefford.'

There was a momentary silence before Dr Rawley said, 'Well, I'm glad he was a satisfied customer. Before . . . what happened to him.'

'Very sad.'

'Yes.' The doctor seemed to feel that enough had been said on that subject. 'So, the question I'm sure you want to ask is: What do we do about it?'

'What do we do about what?' asked Carole, whose mind had been developing other scenarios.

'Your knee.'

'Ah. My knee. Yes.'

'That is, after all, why you came to see me.' Again, a small silence. 'Isn't it?'

'Yes. Yes, of course.' Carole moved into realist mode. 'Well, there's no cure for arthritis, is there?'

'There are many treatments that can alleviate the symptoms.'

'Yes, I'm sure. But there's no cure.'

'Never say never.' Dr Rawley grinned thinly. 'There's a lot of research going on at the moment, so a cure might be possible at some point.'

'When you say "research", do you mean research into new drugs? Or alternative therapies?'

'I was referring to alternative therapies. Drugs have their place in medicine, but doctors rely too much on them. I only prescribe drugs when I have exhausted all other possibilities.'

'Oh,' said Carole. 'And in my case, for arthritis, what other possibilities are there?'

'Acupuncture can be very effective.'

'I'm sure,' said Carole, unconvinced. 'For pain relief?'

'And general well-being.'

That got one of Carole's 'Huh's. 'Any other suggestions?'

'Your manner suggests to me that you don't believe in "healing".'

'That's very observant of you.'

'You mean I'm right?'

'You are.'

'It's not my place to comment on your opinions. I will simply say that I have seen spectacular results achieved by the work of healers.'

Carole was about to say that she lived next to one but curbed the instinct. This was her bit of the investigation. Leave Jude out of it for the time being. Instead, she observed, 'It seems to me that healing is an area that attracts a lot of charlatans.'

'That is sadly true,' said Dr Rawley.

'So, how do you know how to get a good healer? One who's interested in your welfare rather than your cash?'

'It's a difficult area, as you say. You can go online and find websites for thousands of them. All with glowing testimonials. But it's very easy to forge testimonials online. About the only way you can guarantee to find a good healer is by word of mouth. Recommendation from someone who's benefited from their treatment.'

'Hm.' Carole took a risk. 'I've heard, through a friend, of one practising round Fethering . . . called Jeremiah. Do you know him?'

'We have met. I hear very good reports of his work. I'm sure, if you don't warm to the idea of acupuncture . . .'

'Which I don't. The idea that you can cure one part of the body by sticking needles into another part of it is—'

'Yes, thank you, I've heard all of the popular arguments against acupuncture. Many times. All I'm saying is that someone like Jeremiah could give you effective treatment for your knee. Certainly relieve the pain. Would you like me to give you his contact details?'

'No, thanks. I can get them through my friend . . . if I were to decide to go down the route of consulting a healer . . .'

'Which, your tone of voice suggests, is very unlikely.'

'Perhaps.'

Dr Rawley stood up. 'Well, I think that probably concludes our consultation, Mrs Seddon. I have given you a diagnosis of what is wrong with your knee. I have given you a couple of suggested treatments . . . which do not seem to fill you with enthusiasm. If you could settle up with the receptionist on the way out, that would be fine. I would normally say also sort it out with her if you want to book further appointments, but in your case, I don't think that is going to happen. Is it?'

'Probably not.'

'No.' He suddenly looked at her very intently. 'Mrs Seddon, why did you really come to see me?'

Oh dear. She hadn't planned for this. Was he really about to call her out as a fraud, whose not-very-painful knee was being used simply to further a criminal investigation? Carole floundered.

But, before she could give herself away, Dr Rawley revealed that his thoughts weren't going in the direction she'd feared. 'It's a common syndrome that we doctors recognize well.'

'Oh?'

'A patient makes an appointment to consult about some minor condition . . . like, say, your knee . . . and then shows no interest in the treatments we recommend for it. And the reason for that is that . . . it wasn't really the knee they had come about.'

'I'm sorry?'

'Frequently, there's another, much deeper, anxiety that brings them to the surgery. Some life-threatening illness that they believe they may have contracted. Something so terrible to their mind that they daren't talk to their closest family or friends about it. They make an appointment with a doctor either to get the all-clear or to have their worst imaginings confirmed.'

'What, you're saying they imagine they're ill. You mean they're hypochondriacs?'

'Not necessarily. There might be a genuine cause for concern. And their worry about the secrecy of their condition might well lead them to make an appointment with a doctor who is not the one they see regularly . . . just as you have done.'

'Well, I—'

He overrode her. 'Quite often, it's cancer they're really worried about. I just wondered whether that might be the case with you, Mrs Seddon . . .?'

'Certainly not!' said Carole.

*   *   *

The bill she paid to the receptionist was, to Carole's mind, pretty steep. She was glad she wasn't about to book further appointments. But she thought she might possibly have got value for money in terms of information gained.

SIXTEEN

J ude was always surprised what a relief it was to be out of Fethering. The needs of her clients, the concerns of the village, trapped her in an opaque bubble, out of which she could not see the wider world. But being away from the place was like breathing newly minted air. Her life until she settled on the South Coast had been fairly nomadic. Fethering was the place she'd stayed longest. And when she wasn't there, she wondered whether it had been for too long.

The 'Healing Is in the Head' conference in Leeds was fun, and it was a pleasure to be amongst people to whom she did not have to explain what she did. Also, amongst people who did not raise their eyebrows and draw in their breath after she'd said what she did. It was an opportunity for Jude to mix with old friends and be introduced to new people. The programme of talks, panels and seminars had been well thought through, and she was stimulated by the influx of new ideas, which often encouraged her that she was doing something right, but sometimes made her healthily question the way she did things. Such events had often stimulated her to experiment in different areas of healing.

Above all, the conference was an opportunity to spend time with Karen and Chrissie.

The beginnings of Jude's relationship with Karen had been as healer and client. Karen Thomlinson had had everything that in Fethering counted as success – an accountant husband wealthy enough for her not to go out to work, three healthy children at private boarding school and a house on the Shorelands Estate. The only detail that apparently distinguished her from other well-heeled Fethering housewives was that she believed in the powers of healing. Karen Thomlinson had it all.

Yet, when she'd first arrived at Woodside Cottage, she had been so crippled by back pain that Jude had had to help her from the BMW into the house.

Though she would never use words like 'psychosomatic' in conversation with a client, experience had taught Jude that the origin of back pain was frequently in the mind rather than the body. Inner tensions expressed themselves externally. Her healing could ease the physical pain, but nothing approaching a cure could be achieved until the underlying causes had been addressed.

It had taken a long time with Karen, but gradually over the sessions the source of her disquiet emerged. It was her sexuality. As a teenager, she had felt drawn to her own gender but, coming from a very traditional middle-class West Sussex family, she had not allowed herself to give such feelings any expression. They were schoolgirl crushes, just a phase she was going through. Marriage and the demands of children had kept the feelings at bay, but with the departure of the youngest for boarding school, she had been forced to face the reality of her situation. And the conflict between the way she was expected to behave and her real instincts was what had crippled her.

Having identified the problem, it certainly wasn't part of Jude's remit to make recommendations as to what her client should do next. The last thing she wanted to do was to have any part in a marriage break-up. But Karen, having had her own suspicions of what was causing her debility confirmed, felt strong enough to stop having her sessions with Jude and to sort out her own future.

At that stage, there was no female lover in her life, not even any woman who she wished was her lover. But when she finally confronted her husband with the truth, she found there had been a lover in his life. He'd been having an affair with his receptionist at the office for some years.

This made their separation and subsequent divorce easier. And their children welcomed the move. They had been getting increasingly stressed by their parents bickering at each other. Their father married his receptionist and imported her into the family home. With her divorce settlement, Karen bought a smaller house in Fethering, and the children cheerfully divided their holiday time between the two parents.

Karen, away from the stifling conformity of the Shorelands Estate, blossomed. With guidance from Jude, she developed her instinct for healing. It was at a healing conference in Bristol that she met Chrissie, a forty-year-old reiki practitioner from Yorkshire, and from that moment the two were inseparable. In her early fifties, for the first time, Karen knew what it was to love someone.

For a while it was a long-distance romance. They met a lot during term-times, but Karen wanted to be in Fethering for the children during their holidays. Then, when the youngest was settled at university, she and Chrissie pooled their resources to buy a cottage in Ilkley, where, with their different but complementary skills, they ran a thriving alternative health clinic. Soon after Karen moved up north, they got married. All of Karen's children, with their various appendages, were present at the ceremony, and it had been one of the most joyous occasions Jude had ever attended.

She was happy for them. She knew how difficult it was for anyone to find the one person they wanted to share their life with. Given that difficulty, the gender of that person was a detail.

Jude relished Karen and Chrissie's company. They were serious about their work, but not about anything else. Often very funny together, both aware of life's idiocies. And, in common with most gay couples she knew, nothing in their behaviour would have indicated their sexual orientation. If the subject came up, they would talk about it, but they never forced it on people.

The venue for the healing conference was not very grand. Leeds boasted many high-spec conference facilities, but the organizers were working on a limited budget, so the programme of events took place in a converted school. It was somehow in keeping with the alternative ambience of a healing event.

On the Friday afternoon and all day Saturday there had been an intensive schedule of talks, panels and workshops. They had attended as many as they could and, as they sat down in a city-centre pub that evening with a bottle of

Sauvignon Blanc, Jude spoke for all three of them when she quoted a Gary Larson 'Far Side' cartoon. 'My brain's full.'

'Tell me about it,' said Chrissie.

'It's going to take me a long time to process all the information,' said Karen.

'It takes you a long time to process everything,' Chrissie pointed out. 'You still jump every time I refer to you as my "wife".'

'I'm afraid it doesn't seem natural,' Karen confessed. 'Like all those women on Radio Four panel games constantly chuntering on about their "wives".'

'You can take the girl out of Fethering,' suggested Jude, 'but you can't take Fethering out of the girl.'

Karen giggled. 'I've a horrible feeling that's true.'

'What did you think about that feller talking on Rebirthing Therapy?' asked Chrissie.

'Didn't convince me,' said Jude.

'Me neither. I thought he was a bit creepy.'

'Alternative therapies have always attracted their fair share of creeps,' said Jude.

Karen amended that to, 'More than their fair share.'

'Look at us two,' said Chrissie, and they both roared with laughter.

'I thought the guy who talked about Chinese Medicine for Mental Health was brilliant.'

Karen agreed. 'They were so far ahead of us centuries ago. Treating the whole person, not separating the mental and the physical aspects. We've only recently caught up with the concept of holistic health.'

'It's something I've long wanted to explore in more detail,' said Jude. 'I think there are ideas there that I could incorporate into my own work.'

'Me too,' said Karen.

'But . . .' Chrissie interposed, 'we don't want to spend the whole evening talking shop.'

'All right.' Jude grinned. 'So, how's life in Ilkley? For you as a Southerner?'

Karen grinned too. 'Surprisingly similar to Fethering, actually. If I thought there'd be less volume of gossip up here, I was wrong. Everyone chattering away about everyone else all the time.'

'And we, of course,' said Chrissie, 'supply endless gossip-fodder. And behind it all is that great looming eternal question: "What do lesbians do in bed?"'

'To which the answer,' said Karen, 'is mostly read books and listen to Radio Four.'

'Unglamorous but true.'

'But basically, Karen, you like it up here?'

'Love it. Maybe part of it's the company.' The two wives exchanged looks.

'My neighbour Carole believes that people "in the North" are always popping in and out of each other's kitchens, making each other cups of tea. Like something out of *Coronation Street* . . . not of course that she's ever compromised her middle-class eyeballs by watching *Coronation Street*.'

'I suppose it is a bit more relaxed socially,' said Karen.

'Less class-conscious?'

'Don't you believe it, Jude. Ilkley is always about who gets invited to whose parties, who's a social climber and that kind of thing.'

'But, of course, for us,' said Chrissie with mock-loftiness, 'Ilkley is only a staging post.'

'Really?'

'Yes. A staging post on the way to the nirvana of Hebden Bridge.'

'Hebden Bridge where they have all the flooding?'

'Floods are not Hebden Bridge's only claim to fame. Didn't you know, Jude, it is also the Lesbian Capital of the UK.'

'Is it really?'

'Yes.' Chrissie nodded. 'I think we should move there as quickly as possible. Whereas Karen feels . . .'

Karen screwed up her face. 'I think it's a bit obvious. I don't think one should be too stereotypical.'

'Heaven forfend,' said Chrissie. 'You and me – stereotypical!' And they both collapsed in giggles.

Chrissie recovered first. 'But enough of this idle banter. Jude, I know what Karen's really desperate to hear is the latest bulletin from the front line in Fethering.'

'Nothing much changes there,' Jude responded, 'as she well knows.'

'You still got the Fethering healing franchise sewn up?' asked Karen.

'I seem to have plenty of work. More than I can cope with, really. And there is a new kid on the block called Jeremiah, who's keen to set up some kind of centre for a lot of therapists to operate out of the same premises.'

'That kind of thing can work very well,' said Chrissie. 'Particularly for people who're just starting out. When I first qualified, I was attached to a centre like that in Wetherby. It was very good for me. I got lots of tips from the more experienced therapists. And when I screwed up completely . . . well, there was always a shoulder to cry on.'

'But, please,' said Karen, 'I need more Fethering goss. I've been starved of the stuff. So . . . no juicy murders to preoccupy you and Carole?'

'Well . . .' And Jude found herself retelling the strange circumstances of Bill Shefford's death. It was quite a relief to talk about to it to people who knew little of the individuals involved (though Karen did vaguely remember Bill from filling up with fuel at Shefford's). It was also, in a way she did not quite like to define, a relief to be in discussion with someone other than Carole about it. Jude also found talking the narrative through helped clarify her own thinking on the case.

'Ooh, I like it,' said Chrissie.

'Yes,' Karen agreed. 'Plenty of suspects.'

Jude twisted her lips wryly. 'But still no proof it was murder.'

'No, but it's much more fun if we assume it is.'

'Maybe.'

'This healer guy you mention,' said Chrissie, 'called Jeremiah . . .?'

'Yes?'

'Tall guy . . . good-looking . . . deep voice?'

'That's a pretty good description. Why, do you know him?'

'I did meet a feller like that at another healing conference. I'm talking years back.'

'And . . .?'

'And . . .' Chrissie looked conflicted and exchanged a look with Karen. 'I'm afraid I can't really talk about it.'

'Oh?'

'It concerns a client I was treating at the time.'

'Ah. Fully understand.' It was frustrating, but when it came to matters of client confidentiality, Jude knew the rules.

'Incidentally,' said Karen. 'Some people we knew in Ilkley recently moved down to Fethering.'

'Oh really?'

'Name of Greenford. Adrian and Gwyneth. Wondered if you might have come across them . . .?'

'I know who they are. My neighbour Carole has had more to do with them than I have.'

'Well, if you want some choice Ilkley gossip,' said Chrissie, 'there's plenty about them.'

'I'll just get another bottle. This one seems unaccountably to have emptied itself,' said Jude, rising to put her words into action. 'Then you can give me all the dirt.'

When she was back from the bar and the three glasses were full of Sauvignon Blanc, she looked expectantly at Chrissie, who took a deep breath and started, 'Well, I'm not sure whether this could be claimed by the Me Too movement or whether it's a case of old-fashioned marital jealousy . . .'

'Good opening,' said Jude.

'. . . but the Greenfords certainly got Ilkley talking.'

'Which,' said Karen, 'as we've indicated is not a terribly difficult thing to do.'

'Look, who's telling this story?' asked Chrissie, mock-aggrieved. 'Don't forget your place. You're a relative newcomer to Ilkley.'

'I'm sorry,' said Karen, miming the action as she said the words, 'I will zip my lip.'

'What makes it interesting,' Chrissie went on, 'is that it starts very quietly, with the subterranean rustle of a worm turning. The Greenfords had lived quietly enough in Ilkley with no one knowing much about them for more than twenty years, possibly from when they were first married. They didn't have children. Gwyneth was a quiet soul, but perfectly amiable. Worked in the Vauxhall car dealership. Often seen around the shops, always with a pleasant word for everyone. Not many close friends, so far as people could tell, but a number of acquaintances, with whom she would meet from time to time at coffee mornings.

'Adrian was more of an extrovert. Also worked in the motor trade, selling second-hand cars. Was away a lot for work, it seems, but quite a well-known figure round the pubs of Ilkley. What used to be called a "man's man" . . . don't know if the expression's still used. Seemed most at ease with a pint jug in his hand and a slightly off-colour joke on his lips. Such a stereotype – so many more men like him – that he made as little impression as his wife did. Ordinary people, heads rarely seen above the parapet. That is, until eighteen months ago . . .'

'Nearer two years,' Karen interposed, then shrank from the look of mock-fury that was turned on her. 'I know, because it was soon after I moved up here.'

'Very well,' Chrissie snapped. 'Nearer two years. Anyway, it seems that Adrian Greenford had an affair. Had been having an affair for some while. Not a big deal, you may think, in the scheme of things. At any given moment, I'm sure any number of people in a town like Ilkley are having affairs. And you might have thought, allowing for a bit of prurient gossip, it was nobody's business except for the couple involved. And maybe the third party involved. I'm sure that's how Adrian Greenford hoped it would be.

'Unfortunately for him, Gwyneth didn't see it the same way. As I said, it started with a worm turning, but the worm pretty soon took on dragon-like proportions. "Hell hath no fury", and all that. You hear of spurned wives smashing the contents of their husbands' wine cellars and cutting up their suits. Gwyneth Greenford's revenge was more public than that. From being invisible, she suddenly became very visible. She had leaflets printed, stating that "ADRIAN GREENFORD IS AN ADULTERER", and she took them into all his favourite pubs. The landlords didn't let them stay for long, but enough people saw them for the damage to be done. She stuck similar posters over the front of their house and – the final indignity for a petrol-head like Adrian Greenford – she spray-painted the same slogan over his precious E-Type Jag. Was ever a man so humiliated?'

'And what happened to the other woman? Adrian's mistress, girlfriend, whatever?'

'I don't know where she went. She certainly left Ilkley.'

Chrissie sighed, sat back and took a long swig of Sauvignon Blanc. Her part of the narration was over, and this time she made no objection when Karen picked up the baton. 'It's no great surprise that they moved after that. Adrian couldn't go anywhere in the town without people whispering behind their hands. How they sorted it out between them, who set up the house sale, who decided where they were going to move to, I've no idea. But move they did. To Fethering, of all places.'

Jude looked bewildered. 'But how on earth did Gwyneth do all that? Getting the posters printed, taking them to the pubs, spraying the car. Who did she have to help her?'

'She didn't have anyone to help her,' answered Chrissie. 'She did it all on her own – the revenge of a woman scorned.'

'But how could she have done it?' asked Jude. 'In her condition?'

'In her condition?' echoed Chrissie.

'What do you mean?' asked Karen.

'In the house they've bought in Fethering, High Street, near the parade, just a few along the road from Woodside Cottage, which I'm sure you remember well, Karen . . .'

'Certainly do.'

'. . . Adrian Greenford has had to put in all kinds of ramps and handrails.'

'What on earth for?'

'So that his wife Gwyneth can get around the place in her wheelchair.'

'Wheelchair?' The two other women looked at each other in astonishment, before Chrissie said, 'Gwyneth Greenford had no problems with her mobility. She didn't use a wheelchair when she lived in Ilkley.'

SEVENTEEN

Over the weekend, Carole kept thinking about Jude. She wasn't jealous of her neighbour being at a healing conference in Leeds. She couldn't imagine anything she would enjoy less. She needed 'Healing in the Head' like a hole in the head. And she didn't think being in the company of a lesbian couple would improve the experience for her. But she did want to share the news of her Friday afternoon encounter with Dr Rawley. Calling Jude's mobile was always an option, but Carole – typically – was worried that might make her sound needy. It wasn't as if she couldn't survive a weekend with an empty Woodside Cottage next door. The conference, she knew, finished at lunchtime on the Sunday. Jude would be back late that evening. Catching up with her on the Monday morning would be soon enough.

By the Sunday morning, however, the need to make contact was even more urgent. Carole tried to allay it, by ringing her son Stephen and family in Fulham, but listening to the garbled exploits of her granddaughters, Lily and Chloe, did not work its usual magic sufficiently to distract her. When she'd put the phone down, she knew she was going to give in and call Jude.

But, before she had time to dial the number, the phone in her hand rang.

She answered it and a slightly accented voice said, 'Good morning. This is Malee Shefford.'

The house in which Bill Shefford had lived with two wives was not on one of Fethering's most highly prized roads, nor did it have period charm on its side, but it was far enough from the Downside Estate to be deemed respectable. In the front room, Carole was struck again by Malee's beauty. It was not like the glossy allure of a model photographed in a magazine, but something deeper: an iconic face that seemed to symbolize generations of femininity. Seeing her close to, it was more difficult to judge the woman's age. She could have been anything between twenty and fifty.

The room was meticulously clean and tidy but showed little sign of Malee's influence. It had a slightly old-fashioned air, as though nothing had been changed since the death of Bill's first wife Valerie some eight years before. But on the top of a glass-doored cupboard was a photograph of him. In front was a low vase of flowers. Lit candles in short ceramic holders stood either side. Carole did not know whether the shrine was a reflection of Malee's religion or a personal tribute.

She had been offered tea but refused. She wasn't sure what kind of tea someone from Thailand would drink, and didn't want to risk embarrassment if she didn't like it. Typical Carole.

When they were seated opposite each other, she asked, 'Why did you agree to see me?'

'Because you asked to see me,' Malee replied with disarming simplicity. Her English was very good, with only a hint of an accent.

'Has nobody else asked?'

'Nobody outside Bill's family, no.'

Carole realized this was probably true and considered the implications. While Fethering had been abuzz with speculation and accusation ever since Bill Shefford's death, nobody had directly confronted the main suspect. Despite feeling a thrill at being the first one to make the breakthrough, Carole could not suppress a sense of collective guilt that the woman had been so isolated by the village. And that guilt was increased by the knowledge that race had played its part.

'Well, first,' she announced, with awkward formality, 'I'd like to say how sorry I am for your loss.'

Equally formal, Malee bowed her head and said, 'Thank you. It is not the tradition in my country to show outward signs of grief, but that does not mean the pain is not there.'

'As you can imagine,' Carole continued cautiously, 'there has been a lot of talk in Fethering about your husband's death.'

'I can imagine that. I have not heard much of it, but I can also imagine the kind of things that have been said.'

'What kind of things?' asked Carole, keen to establish Malee's position before she revealed anything of her own.

With a wry, pained smile, the widow said, 'Oh, that I was always bad news for Bill. That I cut him off from everyone else. That I wouldn't allow him to go fishing with Red.'

'Red?'

'An old friend of his from schooldays. They used to go sea fishing every Sunday in Red's boat. That's where he lives, in the boat. Down on the Fether, at the marina. I've no doubt everyone says I stopped Bill from going on those fishing trips.'

The very accusation Rhona Hampton had made to Jude. Though, of course, Carole hadn't been there to hear it.

'No, I am not surprised at anything that's said about me. For Fethering, I am the Wicked Witch of the West.' With a sardonic grin, she added, 'Or perhaps it should be Wicked Witch of the East, in my case. Anyway, in the eyes of Fethering, there is no enormity of which I am incapable. I am sure the expression "gold-digger" has been used more than once.'

There seemed no point in denial. 'Yes, I'm afraid it has,' Carole admitted.

'I knew that would happen from the moment I fell in love with Bill. And yes, it was love.' There was a challenge in the look she cast on Carole. 'Though I do not necessarily expect you to believe that.'

'I have no reason not to,' said Carole, though that was a slight sanitizing of her actual views.

'There are lots of corny clichés on the subject,' said Malee, again surprising Carole by her articulacy. 'Saying that, when you are in love, age is not an issue. Well, with Bill and me, that was true.'

'I have to say, Malee, that your English is extraordinarily good.'

'Thank you.'

'Did you study it back in Thailand?'

'Only a little. But in the hotels and restaurants where I worked there were a lot of English people. I am good at listening. And since I have been in England, I have done evening classes in English.'

'And in book-keeping, I hear,' said Carole, remembering Frankie's fears of being elbowed out of a job.

'Yes.'

'And car maintenance . . .' Carole hazarded.

'That too. There are wonderful educational opportunities here in England. Much better than what was available in Thailand. I wanted to take advantage of all of them.'

'With a view to helping Bill in his business?'

'With a view more to understanding Bill's business.'

That sounded like an honest answer. Carole changed tack. 'Was it a wrench for you to leave everyone behind in Thailand? I've heard that family is very important for people of your . . . erm, in your . . .' Carole fought for the politically correct words, before coming up with the acceptable 'in your culture.'

'You are right. I am very close to my family. The fact that I was prepared to leave them behind and come to a foreign country is again a measure of how deep my love for Bill was.'

'Yes.' Carole wasn't quite sure how to phrase the natural follow-on question.

But, fortunately, Malee saved her the trouble. 'You are wondering whether I have been sending money to my family in Thailand.'

'Well, I, er . . .'

'Do not worry, Carole. You do not have to be hypersensitive with me. I know full well the kind of things that Fethering has been saying about me.'

'Ah.'

'And no, I have not been sending money back to my family in Thailand. I love them and hope to see them soon, but I have not been subsidizing them.'

'"Hope to see them soon"?'

'When everything is sorted out here, I will have to return to Thailand. I think I will be more welcome there than I am in Fethering.'

Again, Carole felt a kind of communal guilt. Without becoming overemotional, Malee's words expressed the pain that her alien status had caused her. Fethering could be a chilly environment for people who did not fit one of its prescribed templates. And Carole could not completely exonerate herself from the kind of prejudice that the village consensus expressed. She couldn't forget the remarks she'd made about 'Mail Order Brides'.

'My return home was meant to be in different circumstances,' said Malee.

'How do you mean?'

'Bill really took to Thailand. When he was out there, he absolutely fell in love with the place. He talked of us living there after he retired.'

Carole remembered Tom Kendrick raising that possibility. 'Did he have a plan as to when he intended to retire?' she asked.

'I would have said yes. He talked about September of this year. He said he couldn't face another winter in England.'

'You said you "*would* have said yes" . . .?'

For the first time in their conversation, Malee seemed uncertain, even a little confused. 'Something happened to Bill in the last few months . . . the last few months of his life, I suppose I have to say.'

'What do you mean?'

'He changed. Up until then, he had been so positive. From the moment we met, everything was positive. He was full of plans for us, plans for our future.'

Carole thought back to the last conversation she'd had with Bill, on the morning of his death. 'Positive' was the last word that could be used to describe it.

'But then, suddenly,' Malee went on, 'round about October, I suppose, his mood changed.'

'In what way?'

'He became very . . . I'm not sure of the right word . . . withdrawn? His eyes wouldn't meet mine. He no longer talked about his plans for our future. It was . . . I don't know . . . strange. I kept asking if it was something I had done, if he was ashamed of me . . . and he said no. I think perhaps it was something from his past.'

'But he never told you what that might be?'

'No. But when I think about it, of course he had lived a lot of his life before he met me. I do not know it all, only what he told me. Perhaps I did not know much of it. It's possible there was someone in his past who was an enemy, who he had reason to be frightened of.'

'Did he act as if he was frightened?' Carole's mind was

already sketching out a scenario in which Bill Shefford was a victim of blackmail.

'Yes, he did. There was something . . . I don't know . . . troubling him.'

'Do you think it could have been something to do with the family? Billy or Shannon or . . .?'

'I don't know. I don't think so. They had nothing against Bill . . . well, except for the fact that he married me.'

'Mm. I heard from a friend who'd heard from someone' – Carole changed her mind about mentioning Malee's mother-in-law – 'that Shannon had wanted to come here to look for a will.'

'Yes.'

'And that you wouldn't let her.'

'Is that so unreasonable?'

'No, you're within your rights.'

Carole clearly hadn't kept all the disapproval out of her voice, because Malee said, 'I'm not trying to deceive her. I've looked all through the house myself. I am at least as keen to find the will as Shannon is.'

'And you've had no luck? Have you been on to Bill's solicitor?'

'Of course I have. And yes, they had been in discussion about the will. The solicitor had sent Bill a draft a couple of weeks before he died. The last thing he heard was that Bill was going to sign it in front of two witnesses and post it back.' Malee looked glum. 'It never arrived.'

'And do you know . . .?' Carole began tentatively.

'Do I know what the provisions of the will were? That's what you want to know, I suppose.' There was an edge of bitterness in her voice as she said, 'That, no doubt, is what all Fethering wants to know.'

'There has been a lot of speculation,' Carole admitted.

'I can put an end to that right now,' said Malee. 'It was something that Bill had discussed with me. His plan was that I should inherit this house, some savings he had – not a lot – a small amount he had in a pension pot and the proceeds of a life insurance policy.' She paused. 'And Billy would inherit the premises and the business of Shefford's Garage.'

'Were you happy with that arrangement?'

'More than happy. I had no desire to deprive Billy and Shannon of their rightful inheritance.'

'Did you tell Shannon that?'

'She didn't ask me. She just asked if she could come to the house to search for a will. When I said no, she rang off.'

'So, what are you going to do now, Malee?'

'In the absence of a will, Bill technically died intestate. That means I will inherit everything. I will then transfer Shefford's Garage to Billy. It will take a long time and a lot of lawyers' fees.'

'But if you were to tell Shannon and Billy that, it would set their minds at rest.'

'I have tried to tell them. But it is a difficult thing to do when they slam the phone down as soon as they hear my voice. Anyway, I am not sure they would believe me. They distrust me, you see. And Shannon's mother hates me.'

What she'd heard from Jude made Carole unable to argue with that. 'Very odd,' she mused. 'I wonder what happened to the will.' Malee shrugged glumly. 'I wonder if Bill got as far as signing it and getting it witnessed . . .?'

'I do not know.' Suddenly the widow looked exhausted. The rigid control she had been exercising over her emotions was under threat.

'And if he did,' said Carole, 'who were the witnesses?'

Another weary 'I do not know.'

'What would you feel,' asked Carole, as a new thought came to her, 'if someone else were to tell Billy and Shannon what you've just told me? About the provisions Bill intended to put into his will? It might reassure them and get them off your back.'

Malee shrugged. 'Why would they believe someone else? Are you suggesting you should tell them? Why should they believe you?'

'I wasn't thinking of myself, but I have a friend who's a . . . healer.' She tried very hard to drain the last drop of scepticism from the word. Long habit made that hard. 'She's treating Shannon's mother. I could ask her to . . . sort of mediate.'

'Do what you want,' said Malee listlessly.

'So . . . a missing will,' said Carole. 'Anything else missing?'

'Yes,' said the widow with sudden energy.

'What?'

'Bill's appointments diary. A green book he always had with him. And I haven't seen it since the day he died.'

EIGHTEEN

Gulliver was lucky. He got a second walk that Sunday morning, a beneficiary of the confidence his owner's encounter with Malee Shefford had engendered. Carole already had so much to reveal to Jude on her return from Leeds, that she wondered if she could gild the lily with one more revelation.

The name 'Fethering Marina' raised expectations that were never going to be fulfilled. Adjacent to the yacht club, where rows of neat pontoons provided moorings for the wealthy boat-owners of West Sussex, the marina had once been the home of Fethering's thriving fishing fleet. But the decline of that industry, hastened, if you believed the sages of the Crown and Anchor, by increasingly adverse EU regulations, had decimated the number of locals who made a living from it. As a result, the manmade inlet off the River Fether where the boats sheltered, had suffered from lack of maintenance which would soon make the facility unusable. The twice-a-day sweep of the tides had silted up the entrance and the wood of the old pontoons was eroded and sagging.

The paucity of boats moored there, however, was a bonus for Carole. There were only three. Two were battened down, their tarpaulins streaked with gull droppings, and looked as if they had been that way for a long time. On the deck of the third, mending his nets, sat a septuagenarian with walnut-shell skin.

'Excuse me,' Carole called out, still emboldened by her success with Malee. 'Are you Red?'

His eyes, buried deep in wrinkles, flashed venomously at her. 'What if I am?'

'My name's Carole Seddon.'

'So?'

'And I believe you were a friend of Bill Shefford . . .?'

This caught his attention. 'I *was*, yes,' he said cautiously.

'You've heard, presumably . . .?'

'Of course I've heard. I live in Fethering. Anyone dies in Fethering, it's impossible not to hear about it.'

'Yes. I gather Bill Shefford used to go fishing with you . . .'

'What if he did?'

'But then Malee stopped him from going . . .'

'Is that what you heard?'

'Yes.'

'Who are you, by the way?'

'I told you. My name's Carole Seddon and I—'

'You told me your name. I meant: who are you who has the right to ask me all these questions?'

'I just—'

'I know your type. Far too many like you around Fethering. With your Labrador and your fancy raincoat. Another middle-class snooper. This place was a lot better before all you lot moved in.'

'I have actually lived here for—'

'I'm not interested in how long you've lived here! All I want is a bit of peace on my own boat on a Sunday morning.'

'I'm sorry. I just—'

Red put down the net he was working on and stood up. He was a lot taller than she'd expected and his stance was combative.

'Sorry. One question,' Carole pleaded.

'What?'

'Was it Bill's marriage to Malee that stopped the two of you going fishing together?'

'Yes. I only saw him once after that.'

'And was that because . . .?'

But Red had moved quickly down into the interior of the boat. To emphasize that their conversation was at an end, he had pulled the hatches closed after him.

Carole looked around. Fortunately, there was no one in sight. No one to witness the embarrassing encounter.

As she walked Gulliver back to High Tor, she decided she wouldn't tell Jude about her visit to Red. No need to trouble her with that. After all, she came much better out of the visit she'd paid to Malee.

To defuse the urgency she felt to ring Jude's mobile, Carole spent the Sunday evening teaching herself how to use the camera facility on her new mobile. She had been dreading the process but found it surprisingly easy. She was soon competent to produce a full still and video record of her granddaughters' visit to Fethering in a few weeks' time.

Carole managed to restrain herself until the Monday morning. She took Gulliver for his usual tramp on Fethering Beach and rang Woodside Cottage as soon as they returned to High Tor. It was not yet half past seven. The bleariness in Jude's voice expressed her opinion that this was far too early for someone to be woken, particularly someone who'd arrived back after midnight from a tiring weekend in Leeds.

'I'm sorry,' Carole lied – she wasn't sorry at all – 'but there's something I really have to tell you. You won't believe what I found out over the weekend.'

'You won't believe what *I* found out over the weekend,' countered Jude. 'I found out things about your friend Adrian Greenford.'

'Oh, I'm not interested in him,' said Carole. Then, after a slight pause. 'What did you find out about him?'

'It's more about his wife Gwyneth. She—'

Carole changed her priorities. 'But I actually saw Malee Shefford.'

'You did?' The awe in Jude's voice was very rewarding.

'Yes,' said Carole calmly. 'She told me what was in Bill Shefford's will.'

'Did she actually show it to you?'

'No.' And Carole recreated the conversation she had had with Malee the day before. 'So, will you do it?' she asked at the end.

'What, you mean tell Shannon what was in the will?'

'Yes.'

'She'll think it pretty odd, coming from me. And I can't begin to imagine how her mother will react. Or perhaps I can, all too accurately. I don't think Rhona Hampton is ever going to be persuaded that there's any good in Malee.'

Knowing Jude's love of conciliation, Carole pleaded, 'It might start some kind of rapprochement between them. Make Shannon at least realize that her stepmother wasn't just a gold-digger.'

'I suppose it might.' Jude didn't sound convinced. 'I think I'll have to get Shannon on her own. Any mention of Malee's name in Rhona's presence will just unleash another burst of xenophobia.'

'See what you can do,' Carole pleaded.

'I'll try.'

'Have you got another session booked with Rhona?'

'This afternoon.'

'The perfect opportunity.'

'Maybe. Of course, you realize, Carole, if this is a murder investigation we've embarked on . . .'

'Please say it is.'

'. . . and if anyone did know Bill Shefford's intentions – you know, that he meant to leave the garage to Billy . . . well, it knocks the motives of a few of our suspects on the head, doesn't it?'

'Yes, I suppose it does. Anyway, do your best this afternoon and let me know what happens.'

'Of course I will. And now,' said Jude, still slightly aggrieved, 'I'm going to make myself a cup of tea and see if I can get a couple more hours' sleep.'

'You do that. Oh, and incidentally, how was your conference?'

'Very enjoyable.' She couldn't keep a giggle out of her voice as she said, 'I'm not sure it would have been your sort of thing.'

'I'm absolutely certain it wouldn't,' said Carole, with some force. 'And how were your . . . friends?'

'In very good form.'

'Good,' said Carole icily.

'Ah yes, and I almost forgot. I must tell you what they told me about Adrian and Gwyneth Greenford.'

Which is exactly what Jude did. Much to Carole's amazement.

Rhona Hampton's palliative care was not exclusively Jude's responsibility. She was also under the watchful monitoring of her GP, which suited Jude very well. It had never been her view that what she did was in conflict with conventional medicine. Though she had achieved remarkable curative results by healing alone, she had always been happy to regard her skills as complementary to more traditional treatments.

As the old woman's pain level mounted, the GP had slowly been increasing her morphine dosage. This was administered by Shannon. Her mother could still manage to take the medication orally, though in time a syringe pump might be required. There was no doubt that Rhona Hampton's condition was worsening but, as her remaining time on earth dwindled, she still never mentioned death.

One effect of the medication was that Rhona slept more. She still welcomed Jude's visits and managed to vent some spleen against her usual targets, particularly Malee, but the outbursts didn't last so long. She was tiring, and the relaxation produced by the healing soon brought her the release of sleep.

This was very convenient for Jude. With her client out of it for the time being, it was quite logical for her to step into the Waggoners kitchen, where Shannon was preparing her children's supper. The kitchen itself was functional rather than modern. No islands. It probably hadn't changed much since the Sheffords moved into the house. Stuck to the fridge door was the usual gallery of children's drawings.

Billy's wife looked up anxiously from the pizza dough she was rolling out. 'Getting weaker, isn't she?'

Jude nodded agreement. She had never believed in sugar-coating unarguably bad news, particularly when dealing with a realist like Shannon Shefford. 'But she doesn't seem to be in much pain,' she said.

'Thanks to you for that.'

Jude shrugged. 'I think the morphine's doing as much as I am.'

'No, you're really helping. She looks forward to your visits. With the GP, it's all done remotely. Mum hasn't actually seen a doctor since she's been unable to get to the surgery. They don't do home visits any more. Mum just talks on the phone to him – or her; she never seems to get the same one. And, recently, I've been doing most of the talking to the surgery. Mum's not really up to it.'

'Remotely or not, the GP does seem to be getting the dosage right.'

'I suppose so. Controlling the pain. That's all that can be done now.' Shannon was seized by a sudden burst of emotion and turned away towards the sink as she said, 'I don't know how I'll manage when Mum finally does go. I'll miss her terribly. I know she can be a bit of a cow at times, and she's horrible to Billy, but I've always loved her to bits.'

'I'm sure she's loved you too.'

'Yes. No worries about that.' She was caught by a new spasm of grief. 'And the thought of organizing another funeral, so soon after Bill's . . .' Her words were drowned in deep, torso-shuddering sobs.

Jude saw an opening. 'I gather Malee was at Bill's funeral.'

'She couldn't not be, could she? She was technically his wife.'

'More than "technically".'

'What do you mean?'

'She was his wife – full stop.'

'All right.' The distinction didn't seem important to Shannon.

'And I gather, at the funeral, no one spoke to her.'

'So? Are you asking me to apologize for that? Feel sorry about it? We're talking about a woman who parachuted herself into our family and ruined everything!'

'Have you ever talked to her, Shannon?'

'Not more than I have to. Why should I? Would you talk to someone who destroyed your husband's future?'

'What do you mean by that?'

'I mean that, until *Malee* appeared on the scene,' the name was marinated in contempt, 'everyone knew that Bill was going to leave the garage to Billy. Now Bill's dead and that foreign tart is going to inherit everything.' Clearly, Shannon could match her mother when it came to xenophobia.

'I heard that you asked Malee if you could search her house for Bill's will.'

'Yes, I did. And she refused to let me.'

'A friend of mine knows for certain that Bill did actually make a will.'

'Of course he did. That's why Malee wouldn't let me look for it.'

'Sorry, I'm not with you.'

'Bill made a will leaving the garage to Billy. When I asked to look for it, that alerted her.'

'Alerted her to what?'

'To the danger of me finding it. Nobody'll find it now.'

'What do you mean?'

'She will have destroyed it.'

'Malee?'

'Yes, of course. I should never have suggested that she look for it.'

'Sorry, Shannon, you're going too fast for me here. What are you saying?'

'I'm saying that somewhere in the house where Bill lived for most of his adult life there was a copy of the will he made leaving the garage to Billy. Once I alerted Malee to that idea, she found it and destroyed it.'

'But why would she do that?'

'Oh, for heaven's sake, Jude! Because it left the garage to Billy! If that will didn't exist, Bill would technically have died intestate. I don't know much about the law, but I do know that if a married person dies without a will, the estate goes to the surviving partner!' Shannon leant against the work surface, drained by this outburst.

'You're right about one thing,' said Jude coolly.

'Oh?'

'Bill Shefford did make a will.'

'See? I told you.'

'But he made that will very recently.'

'Oh?'

'After he married Malee. And in the will, he left the house and his savings to her. And he left the garage, the whole Shefford's business, to Billy.'

'I don't believe you but, even if I did, what difference would that make? It would still have been to Malee's advantage to destroy it.'

'She didn't destroy it. She fully supported the provisions Bill had made for her and for Billy.'

'Oh yes? And why should I believe that?'

'You could ask her.'

'Talk to Malee? You've got to be joking.'

'It's better to talk to someone than go around nursing ground-less suspicions of them.'

'My suspicions are not groundless! Malee is, and always has been, nothing but a gold-digger!'

'But you can't—'

Jude was interrupted by a weak voice from the front room calling, 'Shannon.'

Instantly, daughter went to mother. Jude followed, asking, 'Is there anything more I can do for you, Rhona?'

'No, I just want Shannon,' said the old woman with a note of petulance. 'I don't trust healers! They don't do any good for people. Just get them worried about things they don't need to worry about. They're all rubbish. The first one you brought to me, Shannon, he was rubbish. And this woman's no better!'

The sudden change of attitude hit Jude like a slap in the face. Though Rhona had expressed scepticism of the healing profession at their first meeting, there had been no criticism voiced since then. Jude wondered whether the old woman's mind was starting to go. She had been aware recently of a tendency towards rambling.

But this was no time to take issue or defend herself. Jude picked up her woven straw basket and said, 'Very well, I'll be on my way then. See you, Shannon.'

Shannon, who was cradling her mother's frail body like a baby's, hardly seem to register Jude's departure. Just before the front door closed behind her, she heard Shannon calling upstairs, 'Supper in ten minutes, kids!'

The perfect example of the sandwich generation, caught

between the aging and the young. Though Jude feared that Shannon Shefford's sandwich would very soon be reduced to one slice of bread.

As she walked back to Woodside Cottage, she kept asking herself, 'Why won't people talk to each other?' She knew of many situations, usually within families, of conversational lockdowns, which sometimes lasted for decades. And it was her view every complexity in life could be improved by at least talking about it. (Except, of course, for telling a spouse that his or her partner was having an affair. That never helped.)

NINETEEN

'Is this seat taken?'

Carole looked up at the familiar bulky outline of Adrian Greenford, holding his customary mug of flat white.

'No, it isn't,' she said, draining her Americano, 'but get them to put that into a takeaway cup. We need to talk outside.'

'Really? Surely I—?'

By then Carole had left Starbucks.

He found her in one of the seafront shelters facing Fethering Beach. Though full of day trippers in the summer, they were deserted in February. The cold wind sawed through the broken glass of the windows.

He sat down on the paint-denuded wooden seat beside her, a respectable distance away. 'So, what's all this about, Carole? Very mysterious.' His tone was joshing, ready to join in whatever game she was up to.

'It's about your wife.'

'Oh?' A new alertness came into his manner. 'What's Gwyneth done to annoy you?'

'I'm not sure that she's done anything to annoy me. But there are things about her behaviour that require some explanation.'

'Like what?' he asked, unsure of his ground.

'My neighbour Jude met some people from Ilkley at the weekend.'

'Oh,' said Adrian, as if he knew what was coming.

And Carole told him everything that she had heard from Jude, finishing up by asking, 'So? Does Gwyneth need to be in a wheelchair or not?'

There was a silence. Then he said, 'That's a rather difficult question to answer.'

'No, it's not. It's a perfectly straightforward question. Either she cannot move anywhere without being in a wheelchair, or she can. Which is it, Adrian?'

'Hm,' he said. 'The mind works in strange ways, Carole.'

'What, are you telling me her disability is all in her head? Shocked into immobility like some hysterical imaginary invalid from a Victorian novel?'

'It's not quite like that.' He was still holding his cardboard cup in both hands, as if using it to warm them. 'The fact is that Gwyneth is extremely jealous.'

'If she is,' said Carole tartly, 'according to Jude's friends, you've given her reason to be.'

'All right. I'm not claiming to be guilt-free in all of this.'

'And is that why you moved away from Ilkley?'

'Of course it is. After what Gwyneth did, I couldn't stay up there. I had become a laughing stock.'

'So, what made you choose Fethering?'

'It was about as far away as we could get. And Gwyneth had some recollections of having happy childhood holidays in Littlehampton. I thought making a complete change might . . . well, might save our marriage.'

'And how has that process been going so far?'

'Good. Well, good in some respects. Good, in that Gwyneth hasn't gone around vilifying me in Fethering, like she did in Ilkley.'

'You still haven't explained about the wheelchair.'

'No. Well, I'm afraid that was part of her deal.'

'Deal?'

'Yes. Gwyneth made certain conditions when we moved down here. Things that I had to agree to if the marriage was to continue. She's a very powerful woman, you know, Carole.'

'Is she?' came the dry response.

'I'm afraid . . . I'm not proud to say this, but throughout our marriage . . . I've always done what she asked me to.'

'Done what she told you to, do you mean?'

'I suppose so. I wanted to have children. Gwyneth didn't. So, we don't have children.'

'I see.' Carole was glad she hadn't made any comment when Gwyneth had confided that detail to her.

'Haven't you been tempted to leave her at times?' asked Carole. After all, even she had a divorce behind her.

'Oh, I couldn't do that,' said Adrian, as if she'd suggested the unthinkable. 'Gwyneth and I couldn't part.'

'And yet you quite happily went off to have an affair.'

'I don't think "quite happily" would be the best way of describing that situation.'

Carole shrugged. 'Up to you. You still haven't told me about the wheelchair. Is Gwyneth physically disabled or not?'

'She might as well be.'

'What kind of an answer's that?'

'I mean that was one of the conditions she made when moving down here. That she would be in a wheelchair and I would do everything for her.'

'But that's madness.'

'It was the deal. It was the deal I agreed to.'

'Is it her form of punishment for you?'

'Yes.' He put down his cup of coffee, which must have gone cold by now, and rubbed the back of his hand against his furrowed brow. 'My punishment. As I say, she's a very jealous woman.'

'Evidently.' Carole stood up brusquely. 'I think we should probably cease to meet, Adrian. It sounds like you have a lot to sort out with Gwyneth.'

'Yes, I have. But we can't stop meeting.'

'If she's as jealous as you say, she'll begin to think that there's something between us.'

'She already thinks that.'

'What!' Carole was thunderstruck.

'And in a way it's true.'

'In what way?'

'I think I'm in love with you, Carole,' he admitted.

'Oh, for God's sake!' she said, as she strode back towards the High Tor.

Her conversation with Adrian Greenford had given Carole a lot to process. If Gwyneth wasn't actually disabled, if she could move around, and if she was as jealous of Carole as he'd said, then perhaps it was she who had delivered the poisoned pen letters . . .? She could easily have gone out of the back garden gate of Wharfedale to the back garden gate of High Tor . . . God, maybe it was Gwyneth who had smashed the back windscreen of the Renault in the first place?

But Carole wasn't allowed time to pursue these thoughts. Even before she had reached her front gate, Jude had come rushing out of Woodside Cottage to greet her. Carole herself wouldn't have done that. She would have waited till she was back in High Tor, then rung next door to suggest their meeting. But each to her own. She had got used to Jude's impulsiveness. It did still feel rather Northern, though. Maybe it had been increased by her recent visit to Ilkley.

'I had a thought I wanted to run by you,' said her neighbour.

'Over a cup of coffee?'

'Please.'

The Aga gave a degree of warmth to Carole's functional kitchen. It was never going to be a cosy room but, with Gulliver snuffling through his doggy dreams on the floor, it felt almost welcoming.

'My thought was,' said Jude, 'that I should get back in touch with Tom Kendrick.'

'Nothing to stop you. But I'm not sure how much he could add to what he told us in Brighton.'

'I just wondered what interaction he had with Bill Shefford when he brought his car in for servicing. The more we can find out about Bill's behaviour in the days before his death, the better.'

'Fine. It's certainly worth asking. We don't have many other avenues of enquiry open.'

'No. Well, there is another. I was just wondering . . .'

'Hm?'

'Whether you remember anything else significant about when you were there in the garage – you know, the morning he died?'

Carole let out an exasperated sigh. 'We've been through this time and again, Jude.'

'Yes, but there might be some little detail . . .'

'I've told you. He talked about death. He talked about being in a position where something he was going to do would please some people but not please others. Which at the time I thought meant leaving the Shefford's business to Malee and going off with her to Thailand, but now I've talked to her I'm not so sure about that. He was just generally in a low mood.'

'Depressed.'

'I'm sure that's how you'd describe it – depressed.' It wasn't a word Carole liked to use. In her personal dictionary, it had connotations of self-indulgence, of not standing up to life. Deep exploration of such thoughts, in her view, was a kind of navel-gazing. She never rationalized that her vehement dislike of the word might be a way of dealing with her own potential depression.

'Mm.' Jude was thoughtful for a moment. Then, 'Right.' She whipped out her mobile. 'I'll ring Tom now.'

Again, the phone was answered by the gatekeeper of Troubadours, Natalie Kendrick. Again, Jude wished she'd got Tom's mobile number. And yet again, she wondered about the precise dynamics of the family relationship there. Was Tom Kendrick's lethargy and lack of ambition a direct result of his mother's omnicompetence? Did he just not bother because he knew that, ultimately, she'd do everything for him?

'What do you want?' There was an edge of aggression in his voice. He clearly thought that, by meeting them in Brighton, he had done as much as he wanted to do for the two nosy women.

By pointing and mouthing, Jude indicated to Carole that she was going to put him on to speakerphone.

'When we last met,' she said, 'we talked about your time working at Shefford's . . .'

'Incidentally,' he said, 'I can tell you've got me on

speakerphone. So, I gather I'm broadcasting to the other gossiping granny as well, am I?'

'Any objections?' asked an affronted Carole.

'No, no, invite in the whole of Fethering, so far as I'm concerned. They've already said so much about me, a little more's not going to do any harm. And, by the way, you know I agreed to talk to you in Brighton because I thought it might put an end to the gossip . . .?'

'Yes.'

'Well, it hasn't worked. Whenever I go out, it still feels like I've got a big arrow stuck over my head, saying "Prime Suspect".'

'Sorry.'

'I'll survive. So come on, what is it you want now?'

'It just struck me,' Jude replied, 'that you haven't really told us about how you took your car in for repair at Shefford's.'

'Well,' Tom said, as if he was talking to a couple of five year olds, 'my car needed repairing, so I took it to Shefford's.'

'No, I meant what kind of dialogue did you have with Bill Shefford when you took the car in? If, as you said, you'd left his employment in uncomfortable circumstances.'

'Not that uncomfortable. By mutual agreement. He thought I was crap, I thought his job was crap. Fair exchange, you could say.'

'So, no recrimination when you took the car in?'

'No. He didn't want me as his employee, I didn't want to be his employee. But me turning up at the garage as a paying customer . . . that was different.'

Carole could not keep herself out of the conversation. 'Why did you take the car in?'

'Because it had a problem with the gearbox,' Tom replied, with diminishing patience. 'How technical do you want me to be?'

'Minimally,' said Jude.

'All right. Basically, my mother bought me the Triumph three years ago. Mr Kendrick had had one when the model first came out and she seemed to think that I . . . It doesn't matter. She bought me the car. It went OK for a while, then it started to keep slipping out of gear. I thought it was the clutch, took it to Shefford's. Bill had a look at it, said, no, it was the actual gearbox.'

'How long ago are we talking?'

'Three months back, maybe. Anyway, an old car like that, you can't get a gearbox just off the catalogue. Normal parts dealers wouldn't carry them. You'd have to source it from a Triumph enthusiast. Bill said he'd look out for one. He was quite excited about the job, dealing with an old car where he could actually access the engine. He was always complaining that car maintenance was all done by computer these days. First tool you need is an iPad.

'Anyway, a few weeks later he rang me to say he'd tracked down the right gearbox. I could still drive the thing, had to keep my hand on the gearstick most of the time, but I could get it to the garage. Which is what I did.'

'And when was this?' asked Carole.

'It was . . . let me think . . . two days before he died.'

'And did Bill say anything unusual to you when you brought the car in?' asked Jude.

'Nothing unusual, no. We both knew what required doing. We'd talked about it before. Gearbox talk, which I don't think would interest you very much. So, I just parked the Triumph round the back, gave him the key and he told me how long he reckoned the job would take.'

'Did he tell you how much it would cost?' asked Carole beadily.

'We'd discussed that earlier.' Tom sniggered. 'Mrs Kendrick would be picking up the tab, anyway.'

'So that was it?' Carole pressed. 'No further conversation?'

'No, I don't think so. And now, if you don't mind, you've probably wasted enough of my valuable time. Your call did actually interrupt a very good Netflix series I was watching.'

'I'm sorry,' Jude said meekly. Carole gave her a look. She wouldn't have apologized for something like that. 'Sure there was nothing else?' Jude pleaded.

'Oh, I do remember something,' said Tom. 'Just as I was about to go home – walk back to Mrs Kendrick's house, that is – Bill Shefford asked me if I could do something for him.'

'What was it?'

'Witness his signature on some document.'

'What was the document?' demanded Carole.

'He didn't show me. The paper was folded down, so I could just see where he signed.'

'And you did it, you signed?' asked Jude.

'Yes. No skin off my nose.'

'And what did he do then?'

'He said he had to get another witness to sign.'

'Did he say who?'

'He didn't say, but he went straight through to the office bit . . . you know, where Frankie sits and works out what colour she's going to have her hair done and where she'll have her next perforation.'

'And she signed it?' asked Jude breathlessly.

'I assume so, yes.'

TWENTY

Because she had had more dealings with Frankie than Jude, it was Carole who made the call to Shefford's. When she said she wanted to talk, she was told she was welcome to call at the garage whenever was convenient. When Carole added that she wanted to talk about Bill's will and she wanted Jude to be with her, Frankie said they'd better come to her flat that evening. She didn't bluster or deny she knew anything about the will, which Carole thought was promising.

She lived in Spray Lodge, an eight-storey block of flats near the Yacht Club, just where the River Fether met the sea. The properties on the shore side commanded magnificent views and prices to match. Frankie's faced north and was on the ground floor. So potential views to the undulations of the South Downs were blocked by the backs of the shops on Fethering Parade.

Carole had been to Spray Lodge before, but a long time ago.

She'd visited a rather poisonous old woman called Winnie Norton, whose son-in-law had died in suspicious circumstances. Winnie's sea-view flat had been full of exquisite antiques. Frankie's could not have been more different.

For a start, the whole place smelt of cigarettes. It was a long time since Carole or Jude had been inside a smoker's home. They had both forgotten how pervasive that stench used to be.

Then again, the walls in Winnie Norton's flat had been white, reflecting back the sparkle of the English Channel. In Frankie's, all were dark; if not actually black, giving the impression that they were. And all were covered with posters and photographs of pop stars. Carole didn't recognize any of them, but Jude, having been more aware of the *zeitgeist* of the times she lived through, identified them as the movers and shakers of Britpop. Oasis, Blur, Suede, Pulp . . . the in-your-face faces of their members leered down from the walls.

Maybe they reflected a period when Frankie had been a genuine rock chick, but with them time had stopped still. The images now looked as dated – and dating – as Miss Havisham's wedding dress.

Frankie's appearance that evening was almost as bizarre. She wore a sleeveless black lace top over a scarlet bra, and tight leggings in a random pattern of psychedelic neon. Her hair was still in its jet-black phase, and the ensemble was rounded off by glittering gold trainers. With all the rings they carried, her ears seemed to have more perforations than a teabag.

She led them silently through the dark hall to an equally dark sitting room. Here again there were more posters and photographs. Jude noticed that they'd all been professionally framed. Frankie cared for her memorabilia.

She gestured them to a black leather sofa. In front of her black leather chair was a low table. On it were glasses, an ice bucket, a bottle of Captain Morgan's rum and a two-litre Coca-Cola.

'Can I get you something? As you see, I'm on the rum and Coke.'

'Do you have any white wine?' asked Jude.

'Sure. Bottle of Chardonnay in the fridge.' She went through to get it.

Both of them were far too well brought up to say that, though they used to drink a lot of Chardonnay, they had gone off it. While Frankie was out of the room, Carole and Jude didn't say anything, but they exchanged meaningful looks. Both were intrigued. They'd anticipated resistance, an unwillingness to answer their questions, but here was Frankie making the evening into a social event. Carole's eyes darted about the room. They settled uncomfortably on the louring face of Liam Gallagher.

Frankie emerged with their drinks. The Chardonnay was served in goblet-style glasses, with an old-fashioned blue and gold band around their rims. She sat down and raised her rum and Coke. 'Here's mud in your eye,' she said. Like the glasses, the expression felt old-fashioned.

Carole and Jude exchanged looks, settling who was going to speak first, but both were pre-empted by Frankie saying, 'You want to talk about Bill's will. Presumably, you heard how I was involved from Tom Kendrick . . .?'

They made no attempt to deny it.

'I still don't feel guilty about what I did. It was the right thing.'

'Tom,' said Jude, 'didn't know what the document he was signing was. Apparently, Bill folded it over, so just the space for the signatures was showing.'

'He didn't make any secret about it with me. He said, "Put your monicker on this, love. It's my new will."'

'Was that unusual?' Carole enquired. 'Him asking you to do that?'

'God, no. Documents I've countersigned for Bill over the years . . . must be in the hundreds. Particularly after Valerie died. If you live on your own, you often have to get signatures witnessed at work.'

'And did he take the will back after you'd signed?'

'No. He told me to put it in an envelope addressed to his solicitor and post it the next day.'

'And, again, was that an unusual thing for him to ask you to do?'

'Not at all. I do all the office work at Shefford's. Have done for years. Sending out invoices, paying bills . . . anything that goes in the post, that's down to me. Always has been.'

'But I assume,' said Jude gently, 'that in this case you didn't do as Bill told you? You didn't put the will in the post to the solicitor?'

'No,' Frankie admitted.

'Why not?' demanded Carole, steelier than her neighbour.

'Because I didn't think what he was doing was a good idea.'

'And did you know what he was doing? Did you read the will?'

'Didn't need to, did I? I knew what was in it.'

'How? Had you seen an earlier draft or—?'

'No. Well, I'd seen a draft of his earlier will, one he made after Valerie died. Up until then, he'd always assumed he'd go first, so he hadn't bothered with a will.'

'Why did he show it to you, the earlier will?'

'Like I said, he'd never made one before. He wanted me to check through, see it all made sense before he sent off the final draft to the solicitor.'

'And did it all make sense?'

'Perfect sense. He left everything, including the business, to his only child, Billy.'

'And how did you know that the provisions of the new will were going to be different?'

The look Frankie gave Carole made her realize it had been a rather stupid question. 'Because why else would he make a new one? Anyway, Bill said to me when he handed it over, "Must see that Malee's looked after if I pop my clogs."'

'So, you didn't read the new will?' asked Jude, taking on the more conciliatory Good Cop role.

'I didn't need to. He'd virtually told me, hadn't he? He was going to disinherit Billy and give the lot to his "Mail Order Bride"!'

Carole was clearly about to reveal the real provisions of the will, but a small flick of the head from Jude dissuaded her. She let her neighbour continue with the questioning.

'And how did that make you feel?'

'Absolutely furious! After all the hard work Billy had put

in over the years to keep Shefford's going, his Dad was just riding roughshod over him. I couldn't allow that to happen.' Frankie was overwrought. She gulped down what remained in her glass and topped it up from the Captain Morgan's bottle. She didn't bother to add any more Coke.

'So, what did you plan to do?' Jude persisted. 'Did you argue with Bill? Did you tell him what you thought when he asked you to sign the will?'

'No. He could be bloody-minded. If you'd got something serious to say, you had to catch him at the right moment. So I thought I'd just . . . well, obviously not put the envelope in the post . . . but wait, catch him when he was more relaxed and ask if he really had considered the effects of what he was doing.'

'And where did you put the will? Did you bring it back here?'

If Jude had hoped the precious document was about to be handed over, she was in for a disappointment. 'No, I left it in my drawer back at the garage. I knew Bill would never look in there. And I was still hoping for a chance to talk to him about it when he . . . when he died.'

Carole felt she had been out of the action for too long. 'And what did you do with it then?' she demanded.

Frankie looked defiantly from one to the other of them and took a long sip of almost-neat rum before replying, 'I burnt it.' Although no criticism had been voiced, she continued defensively, 'It was the only thing I could do! A matter of justice. There's an incinerator we use round the back of the garage. I used it to burn the will the night after Bill died, when everyone had gone home and I was the only one there. I knew if the revised version never saw the light of day, the old one would still be valid. And Billy would inherit what was rightfully his . . . as he always should have done.'

Carole knew this wasn't true. The law dictated that a new marriage invalidated previous wills. So, Frankie's rash action wouldn't have had the outcome that she hoped for. In fact, it would have made things worse. Had the new will been posted off as his father intended, Billy Shefford would have inherited the business. Malee would have just got the house and savings.

Still, Carole reflected, there wasn't much point in telling Frankie that now.

A look between her and Jude confirmed that they were both feeling the same level of deflation. If Frankie hadn't leapt to conclusions; if she had only read the new will . . . But there was no point in considering such variant scenarios. What had happened had happened, that was all there was to it.

'So, what do you reckon now, Frankie?' asked Jude. 'When we met in the Crown and Anchor with Barney Poulton, you were pretty convinced that Malee set up Bill's death. Is that what you still think?'

'What else is there to think?' But her tone had lost its former conviction. Maybe, with the passage of time, the exact circumstances of her boss's death had become less important. She was coming to terms with a world in which he was no longer a participant.

'You two're trying to find out, aren't you?' she went on. 'What happened?'

Carole, on her own, might have denied it, but Jude nodded.

'Why?' asked Frankie, very directly.

It was a good question. 'I guess we're just intrigued,' said Jude. But that wasn't enough. 'And also, I don't like hurtful rumours going round the village.'

'Hm.' Frankie was silent for a moment, making a decision. Then she said, 'I want to know what really happened with Bill, too. I've got something here that might help you. It's full of stuff I know about. And some I don't understand.'

She had clearly prepared for what she was about to do. She reached down in a purple bucket bag beside her chair, pulled something out and offered it to them.

It was a battered green diary.

'Do you think there was love involved?' asked Carole, as they walked back towards the High Street. Jude was better at observing that kind of thing than she was.

'Oh yes. Definitely,' came the reply.

'So, Frankie loved Bill Shefford,' said Carole.

'No,' said Jude. 'She loves Billy.'

TWENTY-ONE

Frankie had allowed them to borrow the diary, in the hope that they might be able to make sense of the bits she didn't understand. Carole and Jude were very excited. They had talked to a lot of people about the case but couldn't wait to get stuck into the first potentially solid piece of evidence they'd found. Because Carole had got a bottle of Sauvignon Blanc in her fridge and Jude's supply was still sitting in her shopping bag on the kitchen table at Woodside Cottage, they decided they would inspect their trophy at High Tor.

Gulliver greeted them blearily from in front of the Aga with a growly cough. Carole asked Jude to sort out the wine while she dealt with the flashing red light on the answering machine.

The message was from Malee Shefford. Had Carole managed to communicate to Billy and Shannon the provisions of Bill's revised will?

She made an immediate call back with the dispiriting news that Jude had tried but failed. Rapprochement still had no place on Shannon's agenda. Carole decided she wouldn't at this stage tell Malee what had happened to the actual will. Wait until she had talked to Jude about it. The last thing she wanted to do was to generate more bad blood between the widow and Frankie. Nor did she mention the battered green diary that was currently sitting on her kitchen table.

'Oh,' said Malee, 'there is one other thing I have found out since we spoke at the weekend.'

'What's that?'

'I have found that Bill had another bank account.'

'For the garage?'

'No. There was an ordinary business account and a savings account for the garage. The same for us at home. I did not want him to set up a joint account for us. I thought that might encourage the family to see me as a gold-digger. But Bill insisted. So, we had the joint account and a savings account. But the new one I have found is different.'

'How did you find out about it?'

'A statement came through the post.'

'You said it was different from the other accounts.'

'Different bank, for a start. All the others are NatWest. This one's HSBC, and he only set it up last October.'

'Nothing to do with the business?'

'I don't think it can be. All the activity going through it is transfers of money from the joint account to this new HSBC account, and payments going out of it.'

'Payments to the same recipients?'

'There are two different recipients. To one the payment's always five hundred pounds.'

'And how regular are they?'

'Every couple of weeks. Sometimes more often. But there isn't a pattern. No standing orders or direct debits. Just as and when.'

'Presumably it says on the statement who these payments are being made to?'

'Yes. It says "APIPENSION".'

'So maybe he did set up a new pension?'

'It seems unlikely. His pension arrangements were all sorted through a financial adviser Bill had worked with for years. I've called the guy in question and he knows nothing about it. And I've checked through Bill's papers. There's nothing there about an "APIPENSION" – or, I suppose, more likely, an "A.P.I. PENSION". Nothing.'

'And what about the other payments? You said there were two recipients.'

'Yes. There are fewer of the others, but they're for larger amounts. Two thousand, three thousand, that kind of thing.'

'And who's the payee there?'

'"VADJ Trading".'

'Mean anything to you?'

'No. Needless to say I've googled it. Nothing.'

A suspicion was forming in Carole's mind, but she didn't want to spell it out. See first in which direction Malee's thoughts had been moving.

'So, do you have any thoughts about where the money might have been going?'

Malee's answer showed that she shared Carole's suspicions exactly. 'The only thing I can think,' she said, 'is that Bill was being blackmailed.'

By the time Carole had finished the call, Jude had opened the bottle, poured two glasses and was sitting at the kitchen table with hers half empty. Seeing her neighbour's raised eyebrow, she said, 'Had to get the taste of Frankie's Chardonnay out of my mouth.'

'Strange,' said Carole, taking a modest sip as she sat down. 'We used to drink bottle after bottle of the stuff.'

'I find that very encouraging. Evidence that some things – like your taste – can improve as you get older.' Jude grinned. 'I could only hear your end of the conversation with Malee. Very frustrating.'

Quickly, Carole brought her up to date.

'Blackmail?' Jude echoed. 'What would someone like Bill Shefford have done to be blackmailed about?'

'I've no idea.' Carole picked up the diary. 'But maybe something in here will give us a clue.'

Jude moved round to the other side of the table, so they could both look at the same time.

The first thing they noticed was that the book wasn't strictly a diary. It didn't have pages printed with dates, and yet it contained a lot of hand-written dates in Bill Shefford's large, rather childlike, hand. Presumably, it was one in a long sequence of notebooks which he replaced as soon as they were filled and which contained every detail of his business life. The pages of the one on the High Tor kitchen table were interleaved with bills and scraps of paper and its bulk was held closed by a large rubber band. The paper was decorated with a lot of oily smudges.

The first entry was early February of the previous year, some eleven months before. And as they flicked through, the pattern of how he used the book became clear. There appeared to be little personal stuff, except for the occasional note to self on the level of 'pick up a loaf of bread'. Otherwise, it was a record of the garage's business. There were notes about parts that had to be ordered, dates and addresses where cars needed to be picked up for service, customer's phone numbers and reminders of when the MOTs of his regulars were due.

Though on first glance, the entries, scribbled down in biro or pencil, might appear to be random, Bill had a system going that probably worked better for him than using a conventional printed diary. When a directive had been followed or a job completed, the note was crossed out. By that simple means, Bill Shefford had always kept on top of his business.

Once Carole and Jude had worked out his method, they realized they didn't have to check through every entry. Which was just as well, because in places the crossing-out made the original notes virtually indecipherable. The pages were thin and bumpy from Bill Shefford's vigorous scribbling.

'Let's move on to October,' said Jude. 'That's when Malee said he started to get distant from her, wasn't it?'

'Yes,' Carole confirmed, stifling a yawn. She was beginning to think it was bedtime if she was to be up at six thirty for Gulliver's walk on Fethering Beach. 'I don't think we're going to find anything, though. It's all garage stuff, nothing personal.'

'We must keep looking,' said Jude, rather firmly. She was better at late nights than her neighbour. 'This is the only proper lead we've got. Come on, let me fill up your glass.'

'I don't think I should have any . . . Oh, all right.'

Fortified with Sauvignon Blanc, they continued to scan the notebook. 'More cars being picked up . . . More taken to the MOT Test Centre . . .' said Carole, on a note of defeatism. 'More brake pads being ordered . . .'

She was rather beginning to wish that it had been Jude's fridge in which there had been a cold bottle of Sauvignon Blanc. It's very easy to make your excuses and leave from someone else's house. Getting a visitor out of your own without being positively rude is always a trickier assignment.

'Just a minute,' said Jude, her eyes darting across the open pages. 'There's something different here.'

'What?' asked Carole rather grumpily. By the Aga, Gulliver coughed again. She wondered if he was going down with something.

'Look, although there are lots of dates in the book, dates when cars are being delivered or picked up for service and what-have-you, there are very few actual timings.'

'Nothing strange about that,' said Carole. 'When I booked the Renault in with Bill, I wouldn't say, "I'll be with you at eight thirty a.m. on the dot." I'd just say I'd bring it in first thing in the morning.'

'Exactly. And the same when Bill was picking up cars from people's houses for service. We've seen lots of those entries. He'd just put down "a.m." or "p.m.". Same with deliveries of parts and things. He'd put down the date when they'd arrive, not the time.'

'So? I can't really see that this is a very big deal, and I am beginning to get rather weary, Jude, so, if you don't mind—'

'No, look, Carole – here!' Jude's finger pointed to an entry. Though scored through by a pencil line, it was still quite legible. '9 October 3.00 p.m. H.' 'And another one there – see, a week later! And there! And there! Dates, times.'

'And always "H",' said Carole, intrigued in spite of herself.

Jude's finger continued running down the lines and flicking on to the next page. The finger stopped. 'Now that one's different.'

Carole peered across to read, under the pencilled crossing-out: '17 October 10.15 a.m. MOT.'

'That's not strange. The diary's full of dates for MOTs. He kept a record of when his customers' MOTs were due. It was part of the Shefford's service. He always rang me about the Renault.'

'Yes, but none of the other MOT references have got times on them. Just dates.'

'So? One of his customers was pernickety about the time of day he or she could bring the car in – or have it picked up. There's nothing more to it than that, Jude.'

'I wonder . . .'

'There really isn't.' Carole looked at her watch and went all Carole Seddon. 'It's nearly midnight. I don't think we're going to work this out now. Are we?'

'No, probably not,' Jude admitted in a tone of disappointment.

'So, let's try again in the morning. When our minds are fresher.'

'All right,' Jude conceded grudgingly. 'First thing?'

'Well, not my "first thing". Gulliver and I will be down on the beach by seven.'

'After that then?'

'No. Tomorrow's the day I do my monthly shop for non-perishable items at the Sainsbury's in Rustington.' (Some rituals of Carole Seddon's life could not be changed for mere murder investigations.)

'When will you be through with that?'

'Let's say half past ten.'

'Come round to me for coffee when you get back.'

'Very well, Jude. And now I'm afraid—'

'Ooh, do you mind if I take the diary?' Carole's expression suggested that she really did mind. 'You won't have a chance to look at it if you're dog walking and Sainsburying, will you?'

Carole was forced to concede she wouldn't. And on that, Jude finally took the hint and left. With the precious diary.

And with both of them wondering what on earth 'H' stood for.

TWENTY-TWO

Jude was still deeply asleep the following morning when her neighbour and Gulliver strode past Woodside Cottage on their way to Fethering Beach. Carole was limping more. Perhaps it was the angle at which she'd slept. Oh dear, she'd hoped she was too young to have arthritis.

Jude didn't have any clients booked in for the morning, so she made her getting-up routine more elaborate than usual. The eight o'clock cup of tea under the duvet was followed by half an hour's meditation before a bath with essential oils and scented candles. Then breakfast of coffee and toast slathered with butter and honey.

But this was not mere self-indulgence. Jude needed her

mind to be relaxed and ready. That morning she knew she had to think.

She wanted to have clarified her own ideas on the case before Carole joined her.

To aid concentration, Jude made green tea. Then she sat down on the sofa, which was covered by a variegation of throws. She took up a cross-legged yoga position and focused her mind on Bill Shefford's death.

Jude felt as she did when there was a tune she couldn't quite remember. All its elements were there, every note and phrase. She just had to join the fragments of memory together in the right order. Then all would be complete. And it would sing in her mind.

She thought of the various people who had surrounded Bill Shefford. Malee, Billy, Shannon, Rhona, Frankie. All with their own agendas. Was it one of them who was being paid from his secret bank account? What secret did they know that he would be so desperate to keep hidden?

She extended the range of characters. Not people who'd had direct contact with Bill Shefford, but people she had seen over the previous weeks who had discussed the death. She felt sure things had been said which were relevant if only she could work out why. She scoured her memory for snatches of conversation in the Crown and Anchor, observations from Ted Crisp or even the odious Barney Poulton. She tried to read between the lines of Tom Kendrick's responses.

Then of course there were the people who she hadn't seen much of but Carole had. That bizarre couple, Adrian and Gwyneth Greenford. There was enough going on in their lives, Jude felt certain, to fill a good few psychological case studies. But could any connection be made between them and Bill Shefford?

Thinking of the Greenfords made her also remember Karen and Chrissie and the Ilkley tie-in. She was sure something pertinent had been said that Saturday evening in Leeds, but again she couldn't drag it up to the surface of her recollections.

And then, of course, there were a couple of other names in the equation. Was it possible that Jeremiah had had anything to

do with Bill Shefford? He certainly knew Dr Rawley, the man
who Carole had met and Jude hadn't. The man who had apparently been treating the garage owner, and who had signed his
death certificate.

Jude decided it was time to take a closer look at the battered
green diary.

The process was a frustrating one. Convinced that the book
did have secrets to yield, she went through the entries in
much more detail than the night before. Starting at the point
where she and Carole had begun to flick through the pages
to pick up again in October, she checked out everything in
the intervening months. But it was all more of the same.
Records of cars due to be picked up for service, with little
notes like 'brakes making a clicking noise', 'smell of oil'
and so on. Reminders of parts to be ordered, upcoming MOTs,
dates of VAT quarters, invoices to slow payers that had to
be chased up.

There were a few notes taken of web addresses, but those
Jude checked out on her laptop were all garage-related, dealers
of cars and parts for them.

Still, the only entries that didn't conform remained the timed
references to 'H' and the one timed MOT. Though she was
coming round to Carole's view that there was nothing sinister
about the latter.

Jude checked her watch. Twenty-five past ten. She had heard
the Renault arrive next door some quarter of an hour before,
but knew that Carole wouldn't arrive until the dot of the
appointed hour. That was just how Carole Seddon worked.

Oh, well, might be worth having another look at the entries
right at the beginning of the diary. They'd flicked fairly
randomly through February and March, at that stage just trying
to establish how Bill had organized the contents.

On the first page she saw something that hadn't caught their
attention before. Through the crossing-out, it read: 'Organize
insurance on SAAB for M.'

Car-related yes – that's why it hadn't registered – but
personal too. He must have started this particular diary almost
immediately after he'd come back from Thailand with his new

bride-to-be. And he needed to add her to the insurance so that she could drive his car. Presumably until he'd organized another vehicle for her personal use.

OK, not of major importance but intriguing. Jude looked with renewed interest at the next couple of pages.

And she saw another entry that wasn't work-related. Scratched through with a dash of biro, it still read quite clearly, 'Get bait for Sunday.'

Just at that moment, the front doorbell rang and she let Carole in. Before even offering coffee, she pointed out her discovery.

'I don't see why that's so important,' said Carole, a little sniffily.

'It's important because I remember Rhona telling me that every Sunday Bill used to go fishing with his mate Red.'

'Oh, really?'

Jude couldn't imagine why her neighbour was looking so uncomfortable.

'But Rhona,' she went on, 'said that Malee put paid to those fishing trips. She wouldn't allow Bill to go. And yet, here he is, after getting back from Thailand with Malee, and he's reminding himself that he needs to get bait for the Sunday.'

'Maybe it was after that that Malee put her foot down.'

'Maybe, Carole. But it's still worth investigating. This guy Red had known Bill all his life. He might be able to give us some useful background on him.'

'Possibly.'

'Now, I wonder how we can get in touch with him. Billy or Shannon will probably have a contact number.'

'Actually,' said Carole in a small voice, 'I know where you can find him.'

Jude went on her own to search out Red. Carole, still embarrassed by her failed encounter, had said, 'I'm sure you're more likely to get through to him with your *natural empathy*.' Only Carole Seddon could make those two words sound like an accusation.

It was sunny for February but nippy. Still only three boats were moored in the so-called marina. Jude was very aware of the smell: salt sea with undertones of diesel oil and rotting vegetation.

Red was once again sitting there, on the transom box by the outboard, going through the elaborate process of rolling a matchstick-thin cigarette. He had clocked Jude's arrival on the pontoon but did not look up until he'd put the fag in his mouth and lit it with a disposable lighter. His expression was as unwelcoming as Carole had led her to expect.

'What do you want? Are you from the council?'

'No. My name's Jude and I—'

'I don't care what your name is. Why're you here?'

Jude had prepared the line she was going to take. 'I've recently been seeing Rhona Hampton.'

The effect of the name instantaneously softened his manner. 'Oh. You a friend of hers then?'

'I've been treating her for a medical condition.' She avoided the word 'healer', in case he was one of those people who would be put off by it.

'Oh?' Alarm wrinkled his face even more. 'You haven't come to tell me she's popped her clogs, have you? I'd heard the old girl was in a bad way, but—'

'No, no,' Jude reassured him. 'She's still with us, but I'm afraid I don't think it'll be long.'

'I'd heard that, and all.' He half-rose from the transom box and indicated one of the side benches. 'Why don't you come on board?'

As lightly as someone of her bulk could, Jude stepped over the gunwale and sat down.

'Could I get you a cup of tea or . . .?'

'No thanks,' she said, having caught a glimpse through the hatch of the boat's chaotically grubby interior.

'So, what is it you're doing for Rhona then?'

Now she dared to use the word. 'I'm a healer. I'm just sort of helping with the palliative care, reducing her pain levels, doing what I can, really.'

'Oh, right. Bill's daughter-in-law Shannon, she's into all that healing stuff, isn't she?'

'Yes. It was she who got me in for Rhona.'

'That would figure. She was always recommending healers

for everything. Anyone feeling a bit gippy, Shannon'd be sending them off to a bloody healer.'

'Anyway, Rhona's been talking about you.' Which was true. 'She told me once how much she misses seeing you.' Which was also true. 'Says she'd love it if you came to see her.' Which was a slight finessing of the truth but, Jude reckoned, justifiable in the circumstances.

'Yes, I would like to see the old biddy before she . . . you know. Maybe I'll give Billy a call and suggest going up to Waggoners.'

'I'm sure Rhona would appreciate it.' Preparing to move the subject on, Jude looked across the still water of the marina to where the tidal River Fether rushed towards the English Channel. 'Lovely spot you've got here, haven't you?'

'Oh yeah, it *looks* all right,' he conceded. 'Looked a lot better when this was full of boats. When Fethering had a fishing fleet. But that's all gone now. Bloody EU regulations. Then we get out of the EU and things don't look any better. And if it's not the EU harassing us, it's the bloody council, wanting Fethering to be more developed for holidaymakers. Holidaymakers – huh. More crazy golf and slot machines is what that means. And nobody cares about us lot who've worked here all our lives.'

He sighed. 'I'm the last professional fisherman in Fethering. When I pop my clogs, that'll be the end of it.'

'But you still do go out fishing?'

'Yes, but not so much. I just supply the hut where people buy fresh fish, you know, other side of the yacht club. That's the only outlet now. Not like it was in the old days. Lorries picking up Fethering fish and supplying the whole bloody country. Exports, and all. Those days are long gone.'

He sighed again, spat the last half-inch of his roll-up out into the water and started the laborious process of assembling another one.

Jude's perfect opening had arrived. 'I gather from Rhona that you used to go fishing with Bill Shefford on Sundays . . .?'

'Yes. But that all stopped when he married the Chink.'

All too forcibly, Jude realized what Rhona had meant when she said that she and Red thought 'alike on most things'. She made no comment, however, simply asked, 'So, it was Malee who put an end to your fishing trips?'

'She was the cause of it, yes.'

'You mean she told Bill he couldn't go out fishing with you?'

'No, it wasn't like that so much. When Bill went off to Thailand that New Year, we said cheerio and looked forward to picking up the Sunday fishing when he got back. Then he was away longer than he'd planned but I didn't think too much about it. Early February I get a text from him. He's back in England and are we all right for Sunday? I say yes, and he says he'll pick up the bait.'

This tallied with what Jude had found in the diary.

'Then, on the Sunday he appears, usual time, pleased as punch – and he's brought the Chink with him!'

'What, was he suggesting that she should join you on the fishing trip?'

'No. He'd just brought her along to introduce her. Well, I was shocked. Beyond shocked, I was. I'd known Valerie – that's Bill's first wife – since we was all at school together. And I couldn't believe that he'd be so disloyal to her.'

'She had been dead quite a few years,' said Jude. 'Seven or eight, wasn't it?'

'That's not the point! I wouldn't have minded if Bill'd hitched up with some nice English girl, a local from Fethering perhaps. There were plenty of them interested after Valerie died but he didn't take no notice. That would have been all right, though. But for him to get caught up with a gold-digger . . . a "Mail Order Bride" . . . a Chink . . . I wasn't standing for that!'

'So, it was you who called a halt to the fishing trips, not Malee?'

'Of course it was! What business would it be of hers? You'd have done the same in my position, wouldn't you?'

Fortunately, the question was rhetorical and Red went straight on, 'Bill'd betrayed Valerie's memory – and I didn't want to have anything more to do with him!'

'So that was the last time you saw him?' Carole had reported there had been a more recent encounter, but Jude wanted to see whether Red would volunteer the information again. 'That Sunday in February?'

'No, I did see him again. Not a Sunday. Only a few weeks back. He come here to the boat. He was very low, said he didn't want us to part on bad terms.'

'Rather a strange thing to say, given you'd parted on bad terms nearly a year ago.'

'Wasn't so strange when he told me the reason.'

'Oh?'

'That's why I wasn't surprised when I heard about his death.'

'What did he tell you, Red?'

'Bill said he'd been diagnosed with cancer.'

TWENTY-THREE

When Jude got back to Woodside Cottage, there was a message on the landline from Carole. Everyone else of her acquaintance would have called her mobile. Carole was worried about Gulliver's cough and had got an appointment for him with the vet in Fedborough. She'd be back some time after five.

Then Jude rang Shannon Shefford, who once again sounded harassed.

'I just wanted to ask how your mum is.'

'Weaker still, I'm afraid. She had a bad night.'

'I'm sorry. Incidentally, I met someone today who was asking after her.' Another entirely permissible finessing of the truth.

'Oh? Who?'

'Red, the fisherman.'

'Right. Used to be great mates with Bill . . . until Malee poisoned that relationship.'

Jude now knew that was inaccurate but it wasn't the moment to take issue. 'So, sorry, Shannon, you were saying Rhona had a bad night . . .'

'Yes. I was up trying to settle her for hours. And her mind's wandering. She keeps talking about things that happened a long time ago and then getting very angry and shouting about people who've never done her any harm.'

It wasn't the moment to say it, but this news did actually make Jude feel better about the way, at their last meeting, Rhona had ripped into her and the whole healing profession.

'Shannon, I was just remembering something you said to me, you know, when you first got in touch.'

'Oh?'

'When you asked me if I thought healing would help your mum.'

'I knew it would. And it has done. I've always been a great believer in alternative therapies. I'd recommend them to anyone.'

'Yes. I was wondering . . . did you ever recommend them to your father-in-law?'

'Bill? I could've recommended what I liked to him, but he'd never listen.'

'Did he ever say to you that he wasn't feeling well?'

'No. He wasn't that sort. He was of the generation that kept things to themselves. He'd never have talked about his health worries to anyone – and certainly not me.'

'Did you notice any change in his health over the last . . . I don't know, the last year, say?'

'I noticed a change in *him*. I don't know that I'd say it was his health. You have to remember I wasn't seeing much of him round then. Hadn't seen much of him since he married *that woman.*'

'No. But when you say he changed . . . in what way?'

'He just seemed to get a bit gloomy and preoccupied.'

'And when did this happen?'

'I suppose in the autumn.' Check, thought Jude.

'And what did you think was wrong with him?'

'Nothing physical. Well, he used to get indigestion a lot, but I think that was just because he ate so many meals on the go, you know, at the garage. Not stopping, just cramming a sandwich or a piece of pizza into his mouth.'

'You don't think he was worried about the stomach trouble? That that's what changed his mood?'

'No. I just think he'd finally realized what a monumental cock-up he'd made by marrying that woman.' Like her mother, Shannon deliberately avoided the use of Malee's name, as if speaking it out loud would give the new wife a status she did not deserve.

'When the excitement of starting afresh wore off . . .' she went on, 'and I don't know, but I'd also imagine the same thing was happening with the sex – which was obviously what had trapped him in the first place. Men of his age are sitting ducks for women like her. The old blokes think they're getting a new lease of life, a new surge of potency . . . It never lasts. I think Bill just came to the awful realization of everything he'd given up by remarrying . . . Billy and me, the grandchildren, a happy life. It'd be enough to make anyone depressed.'

'Do you think he was depressed?'

'I don't know much about the subject, but he fitted descriptions I've read of depression.'

'And did you recommend any therapy to him?'

'I told you – I could have recommended anything to him, but he wouldn't have listened.'

'Did you actually mention anyone, though, any therapist?'

'I may have done but, like I say, I might as well have been talking to a brick wall.'

'Hm.' Jude was thoughtful. 'Going back a bit, to the first time you rang me . . .'

'Yes?'

'Asking me if I'd help your mum . . . I remember you said that you'd tried introducing another healer to her, and it hadn't worked out.'

'Right.'

'You said you thought it didn't work because he was a man?'

'Yes.'

'And you thought a female therapist would work better for a woman client and a male one for a man.'

'That's what I still think.'

'Did you mention that male therapist's name to Bill?'

'Yes, I did. But, like I say, he didn't listen.'

'What was the therapist's name?' asked Jude.

'Jeremiah.'

Jude put through a call to Karen in Ilkley. There was no reply, so she left a message.

She had a couple of clients booked in that afternoon, one suffering a lot of pain from carpal tunnel syndrome, the other totally disoriented by the menopause. She did her best for both of them. Neither noticed any difference in their treatment, but Jude was disappointed. She hadn't met her own high standards. She was too distracted to bring to bear the total focus she required to be effective as a healer.

It was after half past five when her second client left. Jude made some coffee and went back to her scrutiny of the diary, still convinced it had further secrets to yield. Though other thoughts were beginning to make connections in her mind, the green book remained the only physical piece of evidence she had.

Bill Shefford's diagnosis of cancer did of course change everything. It brought back into the equation the possibility of suicide. As someone who had worked in a garage all of his adult life, he would have had the skills to booby-trap Tom Kendrick's Triumph as a means of ending his own life. And, assuming he got the diagnosis round October the previous year, that would have explained the change of mood that Malee had noticed in him. His life had been going well, he was making a new start, he was happily remarried . . . and suddenly a dark shadow had spread itself over everything.

The other anomaly that the new information might explain was the death certificate. It had been legal for Dr Rawley to sign it off because he had been treating Bill Shefford. Had he been treating him for the cancer? Had he indeed diagnosed the cancer?

It was frustrating. All these tempting random thoughts which needed some overall format or template to link them together.

The telephone rang. The landline. It was Carole, saying she was back from the vet's and would it be all right for her to come round? In her tense state, Jude found this little ritual even more annoying than usual. They were neighbours, for God's sake! Why couldn't Carole just knock on the door un-announced like any other normal human being?

'Something to drink?' asked Jude, as she ushered her visitor in.

'Well, a cup of coffee would be—'

'Stuff coffee! I'm going to open some wine.'

'Isn't it a bit early for—?'

'No.'

While she unscrewed the Sauvignon Blanc (which had been transferred from kitchen table to fridge earlier and was now deliciously cold), Jude asked about Gulliver's state of health.

'Oh, he's fine. Vet checked him over and it's nothing.'

'Was it the cough that got you worried?'

'Yes. It can be a symptom of heartworms.'

Jude didn't know what a heartworm was but didn't bother to ask for an explanation. She was too preoccupied to care about heartworms.

Quickly, she told Carole what she'd learned from Red.

'You're right. That does change everything.'

But before further discussion, Jude's mobile rang. 'Oh, hello, Karen. Thanks for getting back to me. How are you both?'

'In fighting form.'

'Good. Listen, I was thinking back to that chat we had in the pub during the "Healing Is in the Head" conference . . .'

Unseen, Carole raised her eyes to the ceiling. A conversation about healing . . . huh. She picked up Bill Shefford's diary and started to re-examine it.

'Most enjoyable evening,' asserted Karen.

'I agree,' said Jude. 'And it's something Chrissie said that interested me.'

'She's right here with me. Why don't I put you on speakerphone?'

'If you wouldn't mind . . .'

'Hi, Jude,' said the third voice.

'Hi, Chrissie.'

'Or should that be "Hey, Jude"?'

'If you like.' That particular line was an occupational hazard for anyone with her name.

'Anyway, Jude, what can I do for you?'

'Chrissie, it was a client of yours you talked about . . . or rather you didn't talk about much, because of client confidentiality.'

'Ah. I think I know the one you're talking about.'

'It was in connection with this healer I've met called Jeremiah . . .'

'Yes. And I remember I said I couldn't discuss it because it involved someone I was treating at the time.'

'That's right.'

'Karen and I talked about that afterwards and she said she thought I was being over-scrupulous.'

'You were,' Karen affirmed.

'So . . . are you prepared to talk about it now?'

'Yes, Jude. In the circumstances, definitely yes.'

There was a silence. Jude was aware, out of the corner of her eye, that Carole was keying in a number on her mobile phone. Unusual. But whoever she was phoning wasn't there. She appeared to be listening to an answering message. Jude, however, was more interested in what was happening in Ilkley.

Chrissie took a deep breath before she began her narrative. 'All right, I had only just got my reiki qualification. I was working out of this place I mentioned in Wetherby, and a mother brought her daughter along to the clinic. The girl had ME . . . you know, myalgic encephalomyelitis . . .'

'Chronic Fatigue Syndrome,' said Jude.

'That's it. Not that long ago dismissed as "yuppie flu". The girl was, I don't know, early twenties and her mother was at her wits' end. Her daughter was qualified as a solicitor but hadn't got the energy to get out of bed, let alone hold down a job. They'd tried all kinds of therapies, but nothing had worked. The mother had heard about reiki somewhere and asked me if I thought it might help. I told her that I certainly couldn't cure the condition – I was very insistent that she took that on board – but that reiki sessions might alleviate some of the symptoms. And they did. I was pleased. After each session, the client was certainly more relaxed and had a bit more energy.

'I was particularly pleased because, you know, as one of my first clients, I was anxious to do well with her. And so we got into a regular pattern of sessions twice a week for – I don't know – a couple of months, I suppose.

'Then, suddenly one day, she told me she was going to stop coming. She'd been seeing another therapist – something I didn't know about – and he had referred her to a doctor because he thought there was something more serious wrong with her. And the doctor had diagnosed cancer.'

'Poor kid. How did her mother react to that news?'

'Well, this is the point,' said Chrissie. 'She didn't tell her mother. She reckoned the poor woman already had enough to worry about. My client was very optimistic, I have to say, at that stage. She actually felt relieved to have a diagnosis of an identifiable disease, rather than something as vaguely defined as ME. And she thanked me for what the reiki had done for her, but said she wouldn't be coming any more because she was about to embark on a process of treatment for the cancer.'

'What, chemo?' asked Jude. 'Radiotherapy?'

'No,' came the reply. 'She was going to have a course of treatment with the healer.'

'Oh my God!' said Jude. 'And the healer was called Jeremiah?'

'Yes. Whether it's the same guy, the one who's turned up in Fethering, I don't know.'

'Do you know the name of the doctor who made the cancer diagnosis?'

'No, I never heard that.'

Chrissie now sounded quite emotional and it was with trepidation that Jude asked, 'And what happened to the girl?'

'It was a long time till I heard about it.' Chrissie's voice was unsteady. 'You know, neither the girl nor her mother had any more connection with the clinic, and I didn't know them in any other context. And then another client I was treating for ME . . . it turned out she knew the family. She told me . . .' Chrissie gulped down a sob. 'The girl took an overdose of prescription medication. Killed herself.'

'And you don't know whether the course of healing that she was—?'

'I don't know anything else, Jude. Just that she killed herself.'

'And are you prepared to tell me her name?'

'Jodie Flint. Jodie Flint killed herself.' Chrissie cleared her throat. 'That's why Karen persuaded me I could talk about it. Client confidentiality becomes less important when the client's dead.'

After she'd finished the call, she looked across at Carole, on whose face there was a rather smug expression. As she leant across to refill their glasses, Jude asked, 'So which particular cream has this cat got?'

Carole tapped the diary. 'I think, from overhearing parts of your conversation and from following my own logic, I know what the "H" that Bill Shefford kept writing down stood for.'

'Oh?'

'"Healer". All those dates and times were appointments with his healer.'

'You're right! God, I've been so stupid! Why didn't I, of all people, work that out?'

'Well . . .' said Carole, with considerable complacency.

'And Bill spent a lot of time away from the garage, picking up cars for services, collecting parts and so on. He could have fitted the appointments in without Billy or Frankie thinking there was anything odd.' Jude remembered something. 'Jeremiah told me that he'd never met Bill Shefford.'

'So? It seems that he was prepared to lie about a lot of things. Anyway, Jude, haven't you done something similar?'

'What do you mean?'

'Denied knowing people you're treating as patients?'

'Clients!'

'Same difference. Haven't you claimed not to know them because of your precious . . . client confidentiality?'

'I don't think I've ever actually . . .' It wasn't worth pursuing. Besides, Jude read a strange expression on her neighbour's face. 'I've a feeling you've worked out something else.'

'Yes, I have, actually,' came the smug response.

'What?' asked Jude wearily. 'Go on, tell me.'

'I believe I've solved the mystery of the timed MOT.'

'Ooh, aren't you the clever one?'

'It comes from a lifetime of doing crosswords, Jude. Words

and letters are not always what they appear to be.' Carole pointed to the diary entry: '17 October 10.15 a.m. MOT.'

'I've always been crap at crosswords, so you'll have to explain it to me.'

'It's a matter, you see, of what "MOT" means.'

'I know what it means and—'

'There's something else odd about this particular diary entry, which I didn't realize yesterday.' Carole's finger found the relevant mark on the page. 'On the next line, also crossed out, is a local telephone number.'

She held her mobile phone out to her neighbour. 'It's the last number I dialled.'

Jude keyed in the redial and was rewarded by the following message: 'This is the Magic of Therapy Centre. There is no one here to take your call at the moment. Our office hours are . . .'

'"The Magic of Therapy Centre",' she echoed. 'Have you heard of it?'

'I've not only heard of it,' said Carole. 'I've been there.'

TWENTY-FOUR

H is hand was cold as he palpated Jude's generous right breast, but there was nothing sexual in the contact. Dr Rawley knew the standards required by his profession. As it had been for Carole's appointment, his thin body was clad in black.

'And you say it's not causing you pain, Mrs Nicholls?' For the personal details at the Magic of Therapy Centre, she had reverted to one of her married surnames and registered as 'Mrs Judith Nicholls'. At the reception desk she had also done a very convincing performance as a woman unhinged by anxiety. In one period of her varied life, Jude had made a living as an actress, and the experience was not wasted in her current situation.

'No pain exactly. I'm just kind of aware of it all the time.'

She judged finely the tremor of ill-suppressed panic in her voice.

'Hm.' The doctor removed the contact from her breast and washed his hands before turning back to her. 'Do you mind if I just check out a few details about your life and lifestyle?'

'No.' With a little nervous giggle, she added, 'Well, to get one of them out of the way, I probably drink more than the recommended government guidelines.'

Jude knew how to play this game. She'd been the one asking the questions to innumerable clients over the years. And she'd seen enough of them terrified to know how to do it.

'You can do up your brassiere if you like,' said Dr Rawley. She had deliberately worn a front-fastening one, which she now hooked up, before rearranging her top and scarves over it. Again, she fumbled with unsteady hands.

As she answered his routine questions, the doctor made notes on an iPad. It was all straightforward stuff. All she had to do was remember to sound paranoid.

When he'd finished the questionnaire, Dr Rawley put the iPad down on his desk. 'It's a scary disease, cancer.'

'I know.'

'Often scarier in the imagining than in the reality.'

Jude, who knew perfectly well what he meant by that, asked, 'What do you mean by that?'

'I mean that it's still the great bogeyman of illnesses. People worry disproportionately about the risks of developing cancer. Much more than other equally threatening diseases. And the worry particularly affects people who live on their own. Which, from what you've said, I gather you do.'

'Yes,' said Jude truthfully.

'Particularly women who live on their own. And particularly women round your age.'

Jude made no objection to this categorization. She didn't mind being written off as menopausal. She was playing a longer game.

'Have you been worrying about the possibility that you've got breast cancer, Mrs Nicholls? Having sleepless nights over it?'

'I have a bit,' Jude conceded, mendaciously.

'Hm.' Dr Rawley was silent for a long moment. 'As a matter of interest, why did you come here with this anxiety? Presumably, you're registered with your local GP?'

'Yes, but there's always such a palaver there about getting an appointment, and then you might have to wait up to three weeks. I wanted a quick response. I wanted to know for sure whether or not I've got breast cancer.'

'I can understand that. And you were prepared to pay for this speedier response?'

'Of course. Money's never been a problem for me,' she lied.

'I'm glad to hear it.' He looked her straight in the eye. 'And is that really the reason you didn't want to go to the GP?'

'What do you mean?'

'For some people, Mrs Nicholls, health is a very private matter.'

'Yes?'

'Particularly if it's something potentially serious.' She nodded. 'So, some people would rather keep their condition a secret, at least until they've had it professionally investigated.'

'I can understand that.'

'And those same people might prefer not to go to their regular GP with their anxieties, because they'd have to sit in the waiting room, probably surrounded by acquaintances, with all the locals speculating about what's wrong with them.'

'Yes.'

'Are you one of those people, Mrs Nicholls?'

'I think I probably am.' Her voice wobbled appropriately. 'I live just along the coast in Fethering, which is a terribly gossipy place. I don't want everyone in the village knowing what's wrong with me . . . that is, if there is anything wrong with me.'

'Hm.' Again he gave her a very direct look. 'And you do still think there's something wrong with you, Mrs Nicholls, don't you?'

Jude managed to manufacture a sob, before saying, 'Yes, I'm afraid I do.'

He grimaced wryly. 'If I told you it was all in your head . . .'

'I still wouldn't believe you,' said Jude. Which was true. But not in the way Dr Rawley would have understood it.

'All right. Well, the first thing that's important to say is that, if you do have cancer – and I'm certainly not saying you do – the illness is far from the death sentence it used to be. Remarkable advances in treatment are being made on an almost daily basis, particularly with breast cancer. And, increasingly, the role of alternative medicine – or what I prefer to think of as *complementary* medicine – in curing the disease is being recognized. A lot of therapists who would once have been dismissed as charlatans are beginning to be taken seriously. As in many areas of contemporary life, a holistic approach is proving beneficial.

'So, Mrs Nicholls, if I were to find you had cancer, and if you were prepared to let me treat that cancer, then you would have to agree to a course of treatment which involved both conventional and alternative therapies. So, I have to ask you – do you believe in the efficacy of alternative medicine?'

'Yes, very strongly,' said Jude. Which again was true. But again, not in the way Dr Rawley would have interpreted the answer. But then she embellished her statement with some half-truths. 'I have lots of friends who've benefited from alter-native therapies. And one who was completely cured of breast cancer by healing.'

'Good. I'm glad to hear that. Every successful outcome is a small triumph over the sceptics. Well, first I think I must set your mind at rest. I don't want you leaving the Magic of Therapy Centre this morning still convinced that you're suffering from undiagnosed breast cancer. So, would you mind taking your top off for me again and we'll have one final check . . .?'

Jude did as requested, removing her clothes with trembling fingers. Again, his palpation of the right breast was expert. 'I really can't feel anything,' he concluded. 'I think you have to accept you have a clean bill of health there.'

He turned, as if about to wash his hands again, then changed his mind. 'But, Mrs Nicholls, since I suspect that you're the kind of woman who's going to worry anyway . . .'

Jude was flattered that her performance had been so convincing. 'I'm afraid I am. A real worry-boots.'

'. . . then I will just check the left breast to be absolutely certain.'

Her left breast was subjected to the same professional examin-
ation. His fingers touched a spot to the right of the nipple and
then glided on. They came back to the same location. He
pushed gently into the yielding flesh. He repeated the movement three more times. Then he moved round to sit at his
desk.

'I'm afraid,' he announced, 'that I have felt something
there that could be a tumour . . . or, to be more accurate,
something that could be becoming a tumour.'

Jude managed to produce real tears as she mumbled, 'I
knew I'd got it. I've known for months.'

But her real mood was far from sad. It was exultant.

Now Mrs Nicholls's anxieties had been vindicated and she
actually did have breast cancer, she asked Dr Rawley whether
she should have a confirmatory X-ray. He said that might be
necessary in time, but a new technique had recently been
developed which could detect cancer in the system from a
simple blood test.

Accordingly, he dabbed alcohol on to her thumb and with-
drew a sample of blood into a small plastic bottle, which he
sealed and wrote her details on. 'That'll go to the lab,'
he said. 'I'll phone you with the results within twenty-four
hours.'

'And if the diagnosis is confirmed?'

'Then, Mrs Nicholls,' he said with a thin smile, 'we will
embark on the process of getting you cured. For which, let
me tell you, the prognosis is very good. I'll give you the details
when I call you with the results, but basically your cure will
involve intensive therapy sessions with a healer and taking
various prescribed dietary supplements.'

As she walked down to Smalting seafront, where Carole
was waiting in the parked Renault, Jude still felt triumphant
at having her speculation proved true.

But she also felt furious at the abuse of the healing
profession.

'It falls into place,' said Carole when she'd heard about
the consultation. 'When I went to see him with my knee,
he went through this routine about people going to the
doctor's with some minor ailment and not mentioning

the symptoms that were really scaring them. He referred to cancer then. I think he was testing me out, seeing if I'd rise to the bait.'

'Quite possible.' Then Jude said, 'Incidentally, if you'd like me to take a look at that knee of yours, I—'

'It's on the mend, thank you,' said Carole crisply. To punish her for the lie, she felt a painful twinge from the knee as she changed gear.

Jude didn't say anything else on the way back to Fethering. Her mind was buzzing. She now felt sure she knew what crime had been committed. But she couldn't for the life of her work out how to prove it.

Talking again to Red was a starting point. He sounded very guarded as he answered his mobile. Jude didn't think he received many calls. But he relaxed when he heard who it was.

'Couple of things I should have asked you when we met . . .'

'About Bill?'

'Yes.'

'Go ahead then.'

'You said you weren't surprised to hear that he was dead. And I assumed at the time you meant you thought he'd committed suicide.'

'That's what I did think. That's what I still think.'

'And you think he did it because of the cancer diagnosis?'

'Yes. He said he wasn't getting better, the treatment was costing a lot of money, and he wanted it to look like an accident for Malee's sake.'

'So she didn't think she had driven him to suicide?'

'No, no, for money reasons. He had a life insurance policy. There was something in that meant she wouldn't get anything if he topped himself.'

'I see. You knew Bill a long time. Had you ever known him have problems with his digestion?'

There was a cackle of laughter from the other end. 'All the bloody time. Always got some kind of gut-rot, old Bill.'

'And did you ever hear him say he thought it might be cancer?'

'No. It was his diet. He ate badly. His own fault. Never could resist anything deep-fried.'

'Do you know if he ever went to the doctor about it?'

'Never mentioned it to me. We didn't talk about stuff like that. Certainly never went to Fethering Surgery with it, though his daughter-in-law Shannon kept whingeing on at him.'

'Do you know if he ever took her advice, consulted someone she recommended?'

'Not while I was in touch with him, no.'

'In the autumn?'

'Wasn't talking then, were we?'

'Of course not. But he must've changed his mind, mustn't he?'

'How d'ya mean?'

'You said last time you saw him, when he came to say goodbye, he told you the treatment wasn't working.'

'Yes.'

'So that means he was actually having treatment.'

'Yes. But not proper treatment.'

'What do you mean by that?'

'He wasn't on the NHS. He was just seeing some bloody healer.'

Jude curbed what would have been her normal response to that. In this case, she thought Red's response was justified.

TWENTY-FIVE

Carole produced a cheese salad lunch at High Tor. Jude had some but was totally unaware of what she was eating. Her mind was too caught up with fury and confusion.

Carole had very rarely seen her neighbour angry and knew better than to interrupt her thought processes. She almost tiptoed round the kitchen as she made coffee for them.

Suddenly, Jude announced that she was going next door to bring back the diary. 'There's got to be something in there we've missed! And it's still really the only physical proof we've got.' As she shot through the hall, she said, 'Bring down your laptop. We'll need it.'

Carole thought it wasn't the moment to say that she normally only used the laptop upstairs in the spare room. She didn't want to sound petty.

Jude didn't taste the coffee either, as they once again scrutinized the scribbled entries. After about a quarter of an hour, Carole pleaded, 'At least tell me what you're looking for.'

'If I knew what I was looking for, I'd have found it by now.'

'Could you give me a clue perhaps?'

'A clue is certainly what we need. Look, all right, Carole, I'll tell you what I'm looking for. If our thinking so far is right, the five-hundred-pound payments Bill Shefford was making from his secret bank account were for therapy sessions. But what about the bigger payments, the ones in their thousands?'

'We don't know. And have no means of knowing.'

'I think I do know. I think it's for dietary supplements. I was just wondering . . . Bill made a note of everything in here, everything he needed to remember, business and personal. I was thinking there might be a clue in one of the web addresses he wrote down. That's why I asked you to get the laptop.'

'You said you'd been through them . . . and they were all people who either sell cars or car parts.'

'Yes, but I didn't check them *all*. As soon as I'd found the reference to the bait for Bill's fishing trip with Red, I stopped looking. So, look, if I call out the web addresses, you google them and we'll see if we get anywhere.'

Carole's expression told what she thought of the idea, but she didn't like to argue with Jude in this unprecedented manic mood. Carole did as she was told.

The first six unchecked web addresses were like the others. Car dealers. Car auctions. Car parts. But with the seventh, they hit gold dust.

And at that point Jude's plan of action became crystal clear. She told Carole exactly what they would do.

Or rather what she, Jude would do. The case now seemed

to have become a personal vendetta, sidelining her neighbour completely. But again, Carole did not like to argue.

'I think we need to meet,' said Jude.

'Sure.' He'd answered on the third ring. 'Does this mean you've rethought your reaction to my therapy centre idea?'

His voice was still deep and intimate. Consoling, seductive. Jude wondered why she'd ever been fooled by it. Wondered why she had ever found it – or indeed him – attractive.

'Yes, I have thought more about it,' she replied coolly. 'And I really wonder whether the area needs a place like that when we've got the Magic of Therapy Centre so close by.'

'I see.' His tone of voice changed instantly. The charm was still there but there was a harder edge. 'What's this about, Jude?'

'I went to Smalting this morning. To the Magic of Therapy Centre.'

'Oh?'

'Saw your friend . . . colleague . . .? Dr Rawley.'

'Ah.'

'He diagnosed me with breast cancer.' There was no response. 'I'm surprised you haven't heard from him yet. Because I assume you will be involved. In my treatment. At . . . what? Five hundred pounds a session?'

'What are you talking about?'

'I think you know what I'm talking about, Jeremiah. Bill Shefford. Do you deny that you treated Bill Shefford?'

'Of course I don't deny it.'

'You never mentioned it in our conversations.'

'And do you know why? Bill particularly didn't want anyone to know he was ill. And if he had wanted people to know about it, there's no way I would have told you.'

'Why not?'

'Oh, come on, Jude. You, of all people, should know the answer to that. A fellow healer? You know about client confidentiality.'

That stung. But Jude riposted quickly. 'Did you know that Bill Shefford kept a diary?'

'You're making that up. He wasn't the kind to keep a diary.'

'Well, he did, and I have it. Dates of all your sessions.' That bit was true. 'And detailed descriptions of what went on at those sessions, how he felt after those sessions, chronicles of his every mood swing.' That bit wasn't true.

Jeremiah seemed somehow to suspect as much. 'You're making this up, Jude.'

'I am not.' Time to pull out her trump card. 'There wasn't only Bill Shefford.'

'Oh?'

'There was also Jodie Flint.'

'We need to meet,' said Jeremiah brusquely.

'I agree. Come to Woodside Cottage. Seven o'clock this evening.'

TWENTY-SIX

Jude knew the risk she was taking but her anger outweighed the fear.

It had already been dark a couple of hours by seven o'clock when, prompt to the minute, the doorbell rang. She was unsurprised to see that Jeremiah was accompanied by Dr Rawley.

'Do come in. Sit down. Can I offer you anything?'

Both shook their heads as they sank into her rug-shrouded sofa.

The doctor spoke first. He seemed to be the senior partner in their business. 'I did not expect to see you again so soon, Mrs Nicholls.'

'Don't call me "Mrs Nicholls". Call me "Jude".'

'Very well. Jude . . . I gather from Jeremiah that you have been making accusations against us.'

'Yes.'

'I would say, from the legal point of view, that's a very risky thing to do.'

'"From the legal point of view"? That's rich, coming from you.'

'What do you mean?'

'I think there's a law against diagnosing people with cancer when they haven't got it.'

'Are you talking about yourself? And your rather shabby bit of play-acting this morning? I'll have you know that the treatment recommended by me, with Jeremiah's healing assistance, has had remarkable successes.'

'Oh yes?'

'Some of our patients have had a completely clean bill of health at the end of it.'

'No cancer in their bodies?'

'No cancer in their bodies,' he confirmed.

'Hardly surprising when they didn't have any when they started the treatment, is it?'

'Jude—'

'And when did you decide their treatment was complete – that they were cured? When they got suspicious about what you were up to? Or just when their money ran out? There's no way round it. You two are a pair of quacks, playing one of the oldest con tricks in history.'

'I don't think you're really in much of a position to say that, Jude.'

'Why not?'

'Touch of the pot and kettle. Making an appointment with a doctor on the pretence of having breast cancer when you haven't got it is . . . well, certainly immoral. I think a good lawyer might be able to prove it was criminal.'

'I think a good lawyer,' Jude snapped back, 'would have a much easier job proving that diagnosing someone with breast cancer when they haven't got it is criminal.'

'I haven't diagnosed you, Jude. I am awaiting the results of a blood test.'

'Which I bet will be negative now. Anyway, since when has a simple blood test been an adequate proof that someone has cancer?'

'I am afraid, Jude, that you do not have nearly as much medical knowledge as I have. New techniques are being developed every day. I know a lot more about them than you do. And I know that I have done nothing illegal in your case.'

'Possibly not. Yet. But let's put my case to one side. I only came to see you this morning as a means to an end. And, so far as I'm concerned, the exercise worked very well. I got the information I wanted. And that information does not concern me. It concerns Bill Shefford. And particularly the circumstances of his death.'

Jeremiah looked rather nervously at his colleague, but the doctor was unfazed. 'I can guarantee that neither of us had anything to do with Bill Shefford's death. He died in an accident at his place of work. Neither Jeremiah nor I have ever even been to that garage. As I say, we could not possibly have had anything to do with his death.'

'But suppose he committed suicide?'

'That's pure speculation on your part.'

'Would you feel any guilt if he had committed suicide?'

'Why should I feel guilt?'

'It was you who diagnosed him with cancer. If he received the same approach from you as I did this morning, then I would think it very unlikely that he even had cancer in the first place.'

'That again is speculation. And probably slander. I don't deny that I diagnosed cancer in Bill Shefford. I stand by that diagnosis. And since he has now been cremated, there is no way of proving whether or not he did have the disease.'

'But you signed the death certificate that allowed him to be cremated.'

'That is normal medical practice. In a case of unexpected death, if the deceased has not seen a doctor in the previous fortnight, there has to be a post mortem. I had seen Bill Shefford in the fortnight before his death, because I was treating him for cancer. His family had no wish to involve the police or set up any form of enquiry. It was therefore entirely legitimate for me to sign the death certificate.'

Jude should have anticipated that Dr Rawley would have all of his arguments so neatly in a row. She was beginning to feel as though she was on the back foot. She tried again. 'After you'd diagnosed the cancer, do you deny that you put Bill Shefford on a course of treatment with Jeremiah?'

'No, of course I don't deny it. And are you criticizing me

for that? Ooh, be very careful, Jude. You're on dangerous ground here, aren't you? Are you saying that Jeremiah's a charlatan? It's a very small step from that to saying that all healers are charlatans, nothing more than snake-oil salesmen. And then you wouldn't be exactly backing up your own so-called profession, would you?'

For a moment, Jude ran out of steam. Jeremiah took the opportunity to join the conversation. 'You said you had in your possession a diary written by Bill Shefford . . .'

'Yes, I do.'

'In which he writes down all of his thoughts about his cancer and its treatment . . .?'

'Yes,' she lied.

Jeremiah looked back at his senior partner and the doctor took over the reins again. 'I think you'd better give us that diary, Jude. If you do that, then we'll be prepared to forget all about this whole business . . . your making false accusations against us, the risk of slander. I think we're offering you a good deal, Jude.'

'You are in no position to be offering me a deal of any kind!' Driven by sheer anger, Jude's energy was returning. 'I'm innocent in all of this. You're the ones who caused the death of an innocent man and destroyed a happy marriage!'

Infuriatingly, Dr Rawley wagged a finger at her. 'Now be careful. That definitely is slander!'

'I don't care! What I'd like to talk about now is the dietary supplements you foisted off on to Bill Shefford.'

'Dietary supplements?' The two men exchanged anxious looks, then the doctor asked, 'What are you talking about?'

'Do you deny that you recommended him to buy supplements? You were talking about me going on them only this morning.'

'There are lots of medicinal supplements on the market,' said Rawley calmly. 'Just go online and you'll find any number of them.'

'And what about supplements that are *guaranteed* to cure cancer?'

'All kinds of ridiculous claims are made online. Miracle cancer cures have always been out there for the gullible.'

'And what about your own miracle cancer cure? Those

supplements marketed through "VADJ Trading"?' To whom, of course, Bill Shefford had been paying thousands of pounds. And whose web address she and Carole had logged on to this afternoon.

'How do you know about that?' demanded Jeremiah.

There had been a sudden change in the two men's demeanour. She had struck a chord. Both looked uneasy, almost paranoid.

'It's all,' said Jude, 'in Bill Shefford's diary.'

'I think,' said Dr Rawley, rising silkily to his feet, 'that that's even more reason why you should hand the diary over to us.'

'Yes,' said Jeremiah, also rising. 'Where is it?'

'Somewhere safe,' said Jude.

She was amazed by the speed with which they moved. Suddenly, Jeremiah had grabbed her from behind, his large arms immobilizing hers, and Dr Rawley stood in front of her, with a medical scalpel in his hand.

'Where is it?' he hissed.

'It's . . . it's not here.'

'Oh, I think it is.' He raised the scalpel till she felt its touch against the soft flesh beneath her jaw. Not yet a pinprick but capable of being so much more.

'Hand it over, Jude!' Jeremiah's voice was rough now, featuring no finesse, no seduction, just cruelty.

'It's not here. Really. I'm telling the truth.'

'Then where is it?'

'I gave it to my neighbour for safe-keeping.'

Rawley looked at Jeremiah. 'Is that likely?'

'Yes. The pair of them work together all the time.'

'Shall we go next door and get it?' asked Jeremiah.

'No,' said Jude. 'Carole won't let you in.'

'Then how do we get it? I'm sure you know the answer.' The scalpel made a tiny jab. Jude felt it pierce her skin.

'If I ring Carole, she'll bring it round.'

'Oh yes? More likely you'll say something to warn her and she'll run off with it.'

'Would you feel happier if I texted her instead?'

'All right. So long as you let us see what you put in the text.'

At least they had to release her so that she could use her mobile. But Dr Rawley still had his scalpel out. And a tiny droplet of red showed at its end.

'ALL FINE HERE. COULD YOU BRING THE DIARY ROUND?'

The two men approved the content and Jude sent the text. To Carole's old mobile.

It seemed to take forever for Carole to arrive. The two men allowed Jude to sit, but they were restive, moving threateningly around her sitting room. The doctor had not put away the scalpel.

And when the doorbell finally rang, he grabbed her arms behind her back and once again held the weapon to her throat while Jeremiah opened the door.

Which was just as well, because the police whom Carole had summoned when she got the prearranged text signal were able to see the precise nature of the threat being made to Jude.

And, even if they hadn't seen it live, they would have seen it later in the recording that Carole's new mobile had been making from the mantelpiece from the moment Jeremiah and Dr Rawley had arrived at Woodside Cottage.

She'd certainly cracked making the video work.

TWENTY-SEVEN

A couple of days later, Carole was walking with Gulliver on Fethering Beach when she heard heavy footsteps running up behind her. She turned to see a breathless Adrian Greenford.

'What do you want?' she asked, without enthusiasm.

'I . . . Gwyneth said I've got to say something to you.'

'I don't think I really want to hear anything from you.'

'No, please, Carole. She'll really make me suffer if I don't say it.'

'"Make you suffer"?'

'That's what she does, Gwyneth. She makes me suffer. She makes me do things for her. It's because . . . you know, with the woman in Ilkley . . . I hurt Gwyneth so much. That's why she's confined to the wheelchair. She's making me suffer for what I did. And then I fell in love with you and—'

'Oh, for God's sake!' said Carole, now really angry.

'No, I did. From the first moment I saw you, I just knew. But Gwyneth knew too, and she made me do the things . . .'

'What things?'

'The unpleasant things.' Carole still looked puzzled. 'Like leaving the notes . . . going along the alley behind our house, going into your garden and . . .' He swallowed uncomfortably. 'And smashing the glass on your car.'

'*You* did all that?'

'Yes. Gwyneth made me.'

She looked at him, this pathetic man, locked into a marriage whose psychological depths she did not wish to plumb, and thought that, often, there was a lot to be said for divorce. Not, of course, that Gwyneth Greenford would ever allow her husband such an easy way out.

And what made the whole scenario even more ghastly was that Adrian Greenford clearly got some kind of charge out of the situation.

'Goodbye,' said Carole. 'Come along, Gulliver.'

Woman and dog strode over the sand in the direction of High Tor.

Rhona Hampton died soon afterwards. Shannon, who'd always 'loved her Mum to bits', was devastated. Jude went to the funeral. So did Red, who had reacquainted himself with the old woman in her final weeks. A month or so later, he started taking Billy Shefford with him on Sunday fishing trips.

Malee, cheated of her husband's real revised will, spent a lot of money with solicitors, reinstating its provisions. It took a long time, but Shefford's Garage finally became the property of Billy Shefford. He began trying to negotiate with Nissan about the possibly of making it into a dealership for them. They weren't very interested.

His wife Shannon, meanwhile, kept saying it was all point-less because soon people wouldn't be allowed to use cars, thus giving the planet a chance of survival. She thought it very unlikely that either of their sons would want to go into the garage business when they grew up.

Until the change to a dealership came – and there was a strong suspicion it never would come – Shefford's continued as it always had. The elderly residents of Fethering appreciated that Billy Shefford would pick up their cars and return them when they required servicing. And that they could get filled up with fuel without getting out of their cars.

Frankie continued working at Shefford's as she always had. And continued changing her hair colour every month, accu-mulating new perforations and different unsuitable men.

Once the business of the garage had been sorted, Malee returned to Thailand. Carole heard the news some months later on the village grapevine. She felt a moment of guilt for not having been back in touch with the woman, but it soon passed. Carole Seddon wasn't any more racist than any other middle-class Englishwoman of her age and background.

Fethering could be very cruel to people who didn't fit its templates.

Tom Kendrick continued, subsidized by his mother, to do very little.

Karen and Chrissie did actually move to Hebden Bridge, where they continued to be blissfully happy.

The court proceedings against Jeremiah and Dr Rawley, in the way of the English law, took a long time to reach fruition.

The threatening behaviour towards Jude was the unequivocal charge that could be brought against them. The police had witnessed it and there was confirmatory video footage of the attack.

But the false cancer cure they were peddling through VADJ Trading on the Internet came into a grey area of international law which is still not adequately policed. They were made to take down their web presence but it was very difficult to find proof of the actual harm that they had done.

And, of course, their main crime, the misleading diagnosis and treatment which had led Bill Shefford to take his own life . . . well, that could never be proved.

It was a very unsatisfactory outcome, particularly for Carole and Jude. Dr Rawley was given a three-year sentence and Jeremiah, who had not actually used a weapon, eighteen months. There was a move to have the doctor struck off by the General Medical Council, but it was discovered that he had been many years before. Since then he'd been operating illegally under a variety of names, in the USA and Australia as well as the UK. When suspicions built up in one locality, he just moved on to another under a new identity. And presumably Jeremiah moved at the same time. Their cynical scams had been going on for a long time.

After serving probably half of their prison sentences, the two of them would all too soon be out in society again. They would no doubt shift their theatre of operations again, but their evil practices would probably continue. The world will never lack for the gullible and the terrified, searching for a miracle cancer cure.

No action was taken – or needed to be taken – against the Magic of Therapy Centre in Smalting. It was a bona-fide concern which rented out treatment space to various alternative therapists. All those who used it had produced some form of professional validation and the fact that among them was the occasional con artist was not the fault of the centre.

Oh, and Carole finally allowed Jude to have a look at her right knee. It was on their return from a rather boozier lunch than Carole had intended at the Crown and Anchor. The weather had warmed up a bit, she was wearing a skirt and no tights, so there was no issue of undressing. Jude had noticed her hobbling on the way back to Woodside Cottage.

'Let me just have a look at it,' she pleaded.

And Carole, who was in pain and had rung the Fethering

Surgery that morning to be told she couldn't get an appointment for three weeks, made the concession.

Jude did not even get out her treatment bed. She just felt the swollen joint and identified the problem immediately. Dr Rawley's diagnosis of arthritis had been (like so much else in his life) wrong.

'Hm. Have you been doing something recently that involved a lot of kneeling?'

'No, I don't think I – ooh, yes, when I redecorated the spare room a few weeks back, I had to kneel a lot when I was painting the skirting board.'

'And was that when the pain started?'

'I can't really remember but . . . you know it could have been.'

Jude grinned. 'There you are then. It'll soon clear up. All you need to do is take lots of ibuprofen to reduce the inflammation and rest it up as much as possible.'

Carole was very disappointed. 'That's just the kind of thing the GP would have said to me.'

'So? That's the standard treatment.'

'Nothing more?'

'Well, once the swelling's gone down, I could recommend some exercises to speed the recovery.'

'Is that all?' Carole still felt short-changed.

'What were you expecting?'

'I suppose . . . something different from what I'd get at Fethering Surgery.'

'There's no need for anything different. My training and the experience I've gained over the years have given me a pretty good understanding of human anatomy. For a purely physical injury, the treatment I'd recommend is more or less exactly what a GP would offer.'

'You mean' – Carole couldn't keep the disappointment out of her voice – 'no healing?'

Jude giggled. 'What were you expecting – a bubbling cauldron and weird incantations?'

'Well . . .' Carole did not admit that she had been anticipating something along those lines.

'When you consult me about something that needs healing techniques, then I'll heal you.'

'Oh. I think it's very unlikely that I ever would consult you about something like that.'

'So do I.' Jude was having even more difficulty in suppressing her giggles. Through them, she managed to say, 'I do have a stock of ibuprofen if you need some.'

'That's all right. I've got some in the bathroom cabinet.'

'Fine.'

'Oh, but you haven't told me . . .'

'Told you what?'

'What's actually wrong with my knee. What have I got?'

The barrier holding back her giggles burst as Jude announced, 'Housemaid's knee!'

Carole was shamed by the diagnosis. Housemaid's knee? Not only did the very name have overtones of a music-hall joke, it was also extremely common. Carole Seddon would never want to have anything associated with a *housemaid*.

The moment she got back to High Tor, she rushed up to the spare-room office to look up her condition online. She was rewarded by a much better name for it. If the subject ever came up in conversation – unlikely but Carole always liked to be prepared – she would say that she had suffered from prepatellar bursitis. And she would say that it had cleared up of its own accord with ibuprofen, rest and exercise. She would certainly never admit to having been *healed*.

Fortunately, the knee was almost back to normal by the weekend in March when Carole had her two granddaughters to stay. The weather was good, Lily and Chloe were at a delightful age, and they loved scampering around on the wide space of Fethering Beach. They made so much fuss of Gulliver that he thought all of his birthdays and Christmas had arrived on the same day.

The grandmother indulged them all weekend. She took them to the wonderful aquarium in Brighton, where they went through glass tunnels with sharks swimming beside and above them. She also bought them seaside delights like fish and chips and Fethering rock, of which their parents might not have approved. But Stephen and Gaby never knew about these illicit treats because the little girls were sworn to secrecy.

And no fish and chips or Fethering rock appeared in the expert photos and videos which Carole took on her new phone and WhatsApped back to Fulham. But the newly pink girls' bedroom featured quite a lot.

It was a wonderful weekend for three.

The ripples from Bill Shefford's death stayed with Jude for a long time. What hurt her was the harm that the actions of people like Jeremiah and Dr Rawley could do to the image of healing. Every charlatan publicly unmasked did lasting damage to her profession.

And Jude was also starting to get itchy feet. The trip to Leeds had been part of it, but there was more than that. There were other lives she wanted to lead. She still very definitely believed in healing. But she wondered whether she believed in Fethering any more.